Intrepid

Book 6 of A New Life Series

Samantha Jacobey

Intrepid

Book 6 of A New Life Series

Samantha Jacobey

Lavish Publishing, LLC ~ Houston

First Edition
2015 Lavish Publishing, LLC
Book 6 of A New Life Series
All Rights Reserved
Published in the United States by Lavish Publishing, LLC, Houston
Cover Design by: Nicolene Lorette Design
Cover Images: SHUTTERSTOCK
Paperback ISBN
ISBN: **069231993X**
ISBN-13: **978-0692319932**
www.LavishPublishing.com

Table of Contents

Prologue

Enrique ran his fingers around the outside of his mouth, considering the other man's words. "Alright, let's head south. But we gotta be sure we can leave quick, in case she needs us."

"Agreed," Brett grabbed his gear off the table and stood. "Riding in snow is jus' plain stupid, ya know. Ya got your gloves?"

"Yeah, I gots 'em. Hate wearing 'em. They don't feels right."

Brett grinned, "Like frostbite's gonna feel any better."

Enrique followed the older man to the front of the shop, pulling out his protective wear. He stopped to lean on the counter, "At least the wind's died down. We gos straight south from here I guess."

"Yup," Brett swung around, his gaze sliding over the wide expanse of colorful magazine covers next to him. Immediately he did a double take, *what the fuck?* Retracing the path his eyes had traveled, he muttered to himself, *guess I must miss 'er more than I thought… seeing 'er on the front of the tabloids.*

His heart began to pound as he caught the image again. "Hey! We got trouble!" he slapped the other man on the arm

7

to get his attention.

"Man, we always gots trouble. What're you talkin' about?" Enrique chuckled while shaking his head, following the leader's finger as it pointed. Taking in the photograph of the four figures, he gasped aloud, "No fucking way. No way in hells she'd be that stupid." His hand reaching to grasp the issue, Brett fumbled in his pocket to give the clerk another twenty.

Moving off to the side, he flipped the slick pages with his anxious fingers, finding an article about the group. "Oh my God, this's real," Enrique read aloud, *"Tori Anderson, sister of Brian Madson, is joining the band, but can she fill the void?"*

"Well, there goes our plans for some place warm," Brett shook his red curls violently, "Come on, we gotta roll." Swinging around, he headed for the door, "We'll start with that place o' theirs in Jersey."

"Wait! You mean we're going now? Before she even calls us?" Enrique's voice squeaked slightly.

"Yeah, we go now. If anything actually happens, she won' get a chance t' call."

The Band Played On

Tori clenched her fingers, feeling her tenseness ease slightly as they pressed against her mate's. *Deep breath, baby girl. You're gonna be fine.* Smiling at the man next to her, he returned her grin, and she leaned over to give him a small kiss.

"You nervous?" he prodded gently in German, unable to tell by her placid expression.

"Little bit," she replied in kind, "But I think it's going to be ok."

"Sure it is," he gave her hand a shake, "You've got nothing to worry about." He could feel Peter Farside's disgruntled glare upon him as he spoke.

The couple sat in the back of the limo, with the rest of the band in the center, surrounding the bar and enjoying the ride with their typical, boyish banter. Having reached the first week of December, the group has a small gig that will air on a late night program to announce the change in the line-up. The band's newest head of security languished on the far end of the car, only there because Michael had insisted that he come.

Brian took note of her flat calm, nodding his approval, "No sweat, sis. This's a piece of cake," he called out, flashing his teeth for effect.

Everything had been kept hush-hush up to that point, but they knew if they delayed for long, the story would get out somehow. Taking Cody's suggestion to heart, the group had hired a photojournalist, who had taken a spread of pictures for them the previous morning in preparation for the media blitz that would follow the broadcast.

This appearance is the first step; the first hurdle. We make it today, and it's all downhill from here; Tori reassured herself. The photographer had been a real pro, putting the girl at ease and getting a wide range of shots that would be used by various magazines. They in turn would be providing coverage and publicity for the group.

Using an authoritative voice, her brother explained the day's agenda in detail, "The audience isn't very big. And, according to plan, we don't have to do anything but play. That's easy. We go out, do our thing, and we're done." He gave her a small chuckle, happy that things had worked out, and she could be so close.

"I know, Danny. I'm fine. Like yesterday, I got this covered." She smiled at his concern, hoping it really turned out that simple.

Arriving at the studio, the group made their way inside. Tori drew a deep breath, vaguely surprised by the number of people snapping more pictures of them as they exited the car and entered the building. "Wow, I guess I wasn't expecting that kind of welcome."

"It's a fact of life," Collin pointed out in a clipped tone, "Famous people get in pictures. Don't sweat it," he commanded, "You look great." He let the compliment land easily, and it gave Tori a few butterflies that he thought so, considering their past.

The studio being a familiar stop for the band, they were accustomed to the hustle and bustle of the industry, and that afforded her a small amount of comfort. She may not have been acquainted with what would be going on, but the rest of the guys were. If anything wasn't what it should be, they would let her know.

Dropping his bride off at the green room with the others, Michael gave her a small kiss, "Break a leg, baby girl." Leaning his forehead against hers, he rocked her side to side for a moment, "I'll see you after the show."

"Yeah," she exhaled a small puff of air, "No worries, love; I'm fine."

Leaving her, he made his way down the hall, following Pete as he lumbered along. All old hat for Michael, he knew he wanted to have a look at the crowd. Frowning, he stopped next to the man who stood five inches shorter and at least fifty pounds heavier, noticing he had begun preparing a cup of coffee. "You're not gonna have a look around?" his voice dripped with disdain.

Waving his stir stick, the other man replied curtly, "Why? The studio's got security. What's there to be afraid of?" His brow held deep lines, his displeasure at being told how to do his job obvious.

Michael scowled but said nothing, leaving him to his refreshments. Reaching the stage area, he mentally walked through the conversation he had had with Pete the day before. *He has a hands off approach;* he recalled, *putting technology and other people in charge of the group's well-being. With any other band, he might get away with that.*

His eyes made a pass across the smiling faces, and he moved against the wall. Michael didn't like the man's attitude one bit; *he's fat and lazy, in my book. Some things you have to see and do for yourself.* He wasn't ready to ask for his old job back, but he was getting close, the reasons fresh on his mind.

Michael knew that deep down, Tori feared being recognized, and he understood why. *The possibility that it could happen exists, however slim it might be, and that's only part of the danger.* He knew the others didn't fully appreciate those things, but that was ok, he had her back.

Satisfied with what he had seen, he left the spot to make his way around, running into a few of the staffers that he knew. He stopped to shake hands and share passive conversation, and within a few minutes, he had caught up on the news and felt as if he had never left.

Back in their room, Tori joined in the conversation, using the opportunity to mask her growing trepidation at the adventure. "You guys wear more makeup than I do," she teased her brother openly as a young woman painted his features for him.

"Yeah," he agreed with a grin, "Gotta look good, don't I?"

Tori gave her makeup a dubious glare in the mirror and slid into a vacant chair. "So, they do it for me?"

"You relax," the girl smiled as she answered for him, "And I'll have you fixed up in no time."

Tori grinned at the easy way the young woman handled herself. Leaning back into the seat, she maintained her outward appearance, reminding herself that this would be a whole new world for her. All she had to do was follow their lead.

It only took a few minutes to complete the touch ups, and the group was ready to go. Brian sat thumbing through a magazine, and she tried to take her own advice by mimicking him.

After about ten minutes, when it seemed to be taking too long, she demanded in an irritated tone, "How much longer, do you think?"

"It doesn't matter; we wait. Have patience, young one," Brian waved his hand at her, as if he were plying her with some mystical force. The group laughed, continuing to joke with one another and keeping the mood light. Finally, a young man knocked on the door, ready to guide them to the stage.

Feeling her gut tighten, Tori followed behind Collin, keeping herself in check. They walked out to the area that had been set up for them, and for an instant nausea washed over her. She wished she hadn't sworn off vodka as she took her place and strapped on her guitar.

Breathing deeply, she tried to ease herself into the part, but could feel the tension of her muscles while her heart pounded in her chest. Then, moments before they were announced, she caught sight of Michael across the stage, watching from the far side.

He stared at her, smiling broadly. Seeing his quick thumbs up signal and wave, she felt more at ease. Grinning back at her mate, she blew him a small kiss, butterflies briefly fluttering in her chest at the intimate response she had given him.

Closing her eyes, she mentally pushed her fears aside. Hearing the band's name, she opened them to discover that Kyle, the host, had left his seat and trotted across the shiny wood floor, moving towards them. Seeing the camera swing around, Tori frowned, aware that things were about to go *not* according to plan.

Reaching the group, he grinned ear to ear as he accepted a hand-held mic, which he promptly shoved into her brother's face, "So, Brian, tell us about this newest band member. You brought her in pretty quick, don't you think?"

Brian only stared at the man, dazed by the unexpected confrontation.

Trying again, "Do I need to rephrase the question?"

"Uh, no," he managed, "We aren't prepared for an interview. We're here to show off a bit, let you see what she can do." He tilted his head slightly, flashing his famous smile.

"Umm, yeah. We'll only take a minute here, you know, to get some particulars. Maybe you could give us a quick idea of *why* your sister was chosen."

"Why?" Brian played it cool, "Because she's good; that's why."

Kyle only grunted, displeased that he wasn't getting anywhere with the new bass player. Pushing ahead, he added a bit of accusation to his voice, "Yeah, I'm sure she is. However, it's come to our attention that your sister died in a car accident some twenty years ago. Makes it kinda hard for her to play in your band, don't ya think?"

The color drained from Brian's face, and Tori froze for half a second before commanding her brother in French, "Don't answer that." Caught in the middle, he flicked his gaze nervously between the man who grilled him and his sister's clear blue eyes.

With a simple shrug, he tried to bow out of the conversation, "I'm really not prepared to talk about any of this."

Trying to be helpful, Cody cut in, "Look man, we're here to play."

A sullen expression crossed the host's face, and his glare darted to the girl, who gave him an icy stare. He poked the mic towards her, "Would you like to tell us who you *really* are?"

Without blinking, she produced an evil grin, taken with an urge to grab the device and stomp it for him. Shaking her long dark waves instead, Tori shifted her position and gave the count, the rest of the band joining her on cue. As soon as the instruments started to play, the man backed away from her, but she didn't take her eyes off of him as she ran through the riffs and poured her heart onto the stage.

The band played on in true form, and by the end of the

set, they had made it clear that the accident had taken someone they loved, but not their will to go on. Finishing the piece, they rallied up and marched quickly to the side, making their way down the hallway to the back. On the surface, Tori appeared calm, but on the inside she was fuming.

Bursting into their dressing room, she blurted out, "Danny, we can't do this. People already know too much, and it's only going to get worse."

"Come on sis, calm down," shaking his head, he waved her off with both hands, "We don't really have a choice. Either way, the story comes out, whether you stay in the band or not. So you might as well suck it up and get ready for the spotlight."

Glaring at him, the line of her jaw grew tight. *I can't believe I actually agreed to this*; she chastised herself. Her voice choppy with disgust she blustered, "And you don't see this as a problem? I mean, all we were supposed to do was play." She waved her hands, using them to punctuate her words, "You saw the way he came after us. We're the scoop. People are going to be poking around, trying to find out everything they can. They don't *care* about the music; they want the story."

Stopping short, a dark thought sprang into her mind, "You can't tell people what I shared with you the other night."

Brian and the others only stared at her, not ready to interrupt her tirade.

Tori's expression changed into one of bewilderment, considering what she had actually told them. "Some of that stuff's classified," she faltered. "I could get in trouble for saying anything about it."

Shaking his head, Collin cut in, "How can *your story* be classified? It's like, your personal life." He shrugged, palms up, "They can't tell you not to talk about it."

She pursed her lips, considering his words, and then elaborated, "But there are other people involved; other lives that could be put at risk." Seeing he wanted to protest further, she put her hand up to cut him off.

"Please," her voice became submissive, almost begging, "Keep everything I shared with you in confidence. I feel like I shouldn't have done it, and repeating it out in public is going to make things worse."

Clenching his jaw as he glared at her, Collin said nothing more.

Glowering into his eyes, she demanded, "Who'd you tell?"

Wide-eyed with surprise at her deduction, he almost denied the action altogether. Glancing at the floor, he shoved his hands in his pockets. Running his tongue over his upper lip, his gaze slowly rose to meet hers, "I might have given a few details to Mark. I didn't realize it was a secret."

"Holy shit!" Her hands flew to her hips in disgust, "I told you that I had been given a deal by the Feds and gotten away with murder, and you didn't realize it was a secret?" Her voice grew loud, and she practically shouted, "What kind of fucking moron are you?"

Reaching up to lay a hand on her shoulder, Brian tried to calm her, "Let's take it down a notch, shall we?"

Flicking his hand off with an angry twist of her wrist, Tori didn't want to hear it. Using the other hand, she pointed her index finger in Collin's face, "If anything happens to my brother because of this, you'll regret it."

Collin burst into a loud laugh. "Don't threaten me; I'm not buying your *'I'm a badass bitch'* story, ok? So do your fucking job, play the fucking guitar, and don't sweat it. Nothing's gonna happen. It's called *publicity*." His tone mocked her ignorance, "It's what makes people wanna know more about us."

Tori shook her head as he spoke, aware they were in a tough spot due to her poor judgment, and his.

Lowering her hand, she clenched her teeth and stormed out of the room, stomping down the hall. Turning a corner, flashing lights bombarded her, as she had come face to face with a large group of reporters gathered to take photos and try for interviews. Backpedaling, she re-entered the room, and stepped up to the man who had put things in motion, striking him in the face and knocking him back onto the leather couch behind him.

While he dabbed at the blood that streamed from his nose, she leaned over him, returning her finger to its previous position, so close it practically scraped the tip. "Let's make one correction. I am *now* a pissed off, badass bitch," she hissed loudly, "And you don't tell anyone another God damned thing without my say, you got that, you dumb son of a bitch?"

Piles of Money

Collin stared into her fiery blue eyes, wishing he could knock the shit out of her. Unfortunately, she was Brian's sister, and what's worse, he would have Michael to contend with. "Get the fuck outta my face," he replied as he continued to stem the flow from his left nostril.

Straightening, she informed the group bitterly, "There's a large congregation of press outside. We need to get moving, so we're going to walk through them without saying a word." Giving Collin a cold glare, she instructed, "Don't smile, don't wave...walk. We get in the car, and we get the hell out of here. When we get back to the house, we can assess the damage and plan our next move."

Collin didn't argue, but she could tell by his pout he wasn't keen on taking orders from her. Glowering down at him, her lips curled into a snarl, "When we get back to the house, we're gonna have it out." Pointing her hand back and forth between them, "You and me," she snapped. "I can tell you think this's a game. I'm gonna give you the chance to find out the hard way." Twirling around to put her back to him, she made sure everyone would be ready to leave when her husband returned.

Michael opened the door a few minutes later to discover the faint blood smear on the new drummer's face. "Oh, shit," he mumbled, turning his palms to the ceiling and raising his eyebrows as a silent demand for an explanation.

Ignoring the request, Tori filled him in on her plan to get them out without giving anything else away. He glanced back and forth between her and Collin for a brief moment before he shrugged, "Fine with me."

"Wait, where's Pete?" Cody commented, aware that the other man had not wanted to make the trip with them to begin with. "Isn't he riding back with us?"

"Only if he's in the car when we get there," Michael answered in disgust, "Send him a text if you want and tell him to get moving."

Nodding, with fingers bouncing across the face of the device, Cody quickly complied. As soon as the message had been sent, he gave the command, "Alright, let's go."

Moving as a group, the four band members followed while Michael led the way, ploughing through the line of reporters. Glancing back, Tori could see that Collin Graham wasn't following her directions. He wasn't talking, but he smiled and gave little waves to people, leaving him looking like Mr. Nice guy. Blood boiling, Tori kept her features sedate, storing the rage for their confrontation.

Arriving at the limo, the group climbed in to make the trip to their house in New Jersey, their official security personnel nowhere to be seen. Still angry with Collin, Tori stared at him through squinted lids as they rode, the silence of the chamber stifling.

Eventually, Michael asked what had happened, and she broke into a torrent of German, her favorite language when pissed. Her mate listened as she explained that her story had been leaked to Mark, and passed on to God knows who else.

Hearing this, Michael looked stricken. "How could you?" he demanded, his eyes cut over at the guilty party; all he said, but more than enough.

The man under fire drew in a deep breath, his features shifting at the idea he had, in fact, made a bad choice. "Look," Collin blurted, his voice tense, "The media and the public eat this shit up. Crazy stories sell, and we could use a lot of free publicity here; we could make piles of money on this."

Tori cut in, "Money don't mean shit when you're dead."

The remaining band members listened to the debate. Drama had never been a problem for them before, and it seemed hard to decide which side to take at the moment.

The car rolled into the long drive and arrived at the front steps. Collin shoved the door open, eager to get into the house and avoid the confrontation if he could. Scrambling out behind him, Tori didn't wait to make good on her word, giving the slender man a violent shove.

Swinging around, he taunted her, "Oh no, you bitch! No way're we gonna give you any more fodder for your bullshit stories." He rubbed at his nose; the inside caked with dry blood.

Dropping her cumbersome jacket to the ground, she called back in semi-southern, "Wha's th' matta'... you 'fraid you gonna get yo' ass kicked by a girl?" Holding her hands palms up, she made a beckoning motion by curling the tips of her fingers at him. "Come on buddy, now's your chance. You think I'm lyin', come an' prove it." Tori shifted her weight from one leg to the other, calmly waiting for him to make the first move.

Collin danced in a hopping motion, adrenaline pumping through his veins. Looking over at Michael, he pressed for input, "Is she serious? Or is this a game you two play; she picks the fights, and you finish them."

Michael spit out a short laugh, "Man, you take a swing at her, I'm not bailing you out. You're on your own."

The other two members of the group stepped back,

observing that Michael, clearly under the belief that Tori would win if Collin gave in to her challenge, had crossed his arms in disgust. It would be a long shot, they were certain, and the risk of having either of them injured would be too great.

"Hey, why don't you two knock it off," Cody tried to intervene, only egging his friend on.

"What's the matter, you think she can take me?" Collin tossed angrily, slapping his chest with his fist.

Cody raised both hands in surrender, "No, man; I don't wanna see you guys fight, that's all." He tried to smooth things, but Tori stood gaping at her nemesis, and he still hopped about, considering his options.

Finally, Collin made his choice. Dropping his jacket to the ground as well, he stepped forward to throw a legitimate punch, but seeing his advancing momentum sent the girl into action. In a spinning movement, she dodged under his swing, causing the miss while she caught his arm from behind, twisting it and knocking him to the ground.

Landing two blows with her forearm against his head and neck, she kicked his leg out from under him where he squatted awkwardly, and he found himself face down on the dirt.

Pacing around him in a slow circle, Tori clenched and unclenched her fists, waiting for him to try and stand.

Shaking his head to clear it, Collin drew a knee up underneath him, raising his belly and exposing his soft underside. With a quick step forward, she kicked him in the gut, soccer style, knocking the wind out of him and sending him reeling over onto his back.

Rolling quickly, he wanted to get back on his feet, but the girl had no intention of allowing that to happen. Kicking him behind the knee, she elbowed him in the back of his neck for the second time, only this time as he stretched out, and didn't bother to try and get up. Flopping from his belly to his back, he stared up at her. He breathed hard, but Tori appeared an eerie calm.

Standing over him, the girl worked her hands into fists, fighting the urge to plunge her knee into his chest and begin the second phase of her assault. Her long black hair around her, his blood stood out in sharp contrast with her white shirt, the group holding their breath in unison at the sight of it.

Collin licked his lips nervously, aware he either had to concede or continue to take a beating, as Michael had been true to his word and not done anything to help him out. Opening his palms towards the sky, he stammered, "Ok, I get your point." Spitting dry grass from his mouth, he continued, "Can I get up now?"

Tori stared at him for a moment, then spun around and snatched her jacket off the ground. Making her way to the door, she recapped the confrontation in her mind, scoring her moves according to her old system, still amazed at how easy it could be to take down those who had never been trained.

Cody helped his friend to his feet, and they followed the girl into the house. Making her way to the kitchen, she washed her hands in the sink, still placid on the outside. Inside, she could feel the mild rush from the adrenaline she had learned to control. Moving aside so that he could cleanse his wounds, she looked around at the others, who stared at her.

With a small huff, she stated loudly, "We have to figure out what we're going to do. You're right; it's too late to duck and cover. People are already onto the story, and it'll be big news, I'm sure. People don't come back after being dead for twenty years every day." She waited for their input, but they remained tight-lipped, and she began to think aloud.

"Maybe we should decide which parts of the story we want to put out, and flood the media with it." Looking over at her victim as he dried his face, she demanded, "What did you tell Mark? We need to get him over here, right now."

Brian pulled out his cell to call their manager, hoping the man would comply.

A sickening thought occurred to her, and Tori realized she would have to make a phone call of her own. Excusing herself, she made her way upstairs. Pulling her pack out of the closet, she located the go-phone she had carried when she rode with the Scorpions. Stored in its memory she would find James Godfry's phone number, and she needed it to contact him.

Plugging in the device, she waited for it to gain a charge, enough to turn it on and pull up the record. Then she used the house phone to make the call. Hearing his voice on the other end, Tori pictured the short fat man she had first grappled with from her hospital bed.

"Jim?" she kept her voice calm, "Hey, Jim; it's Tori. Listen, I need to find out what you guys did about the little girl who was buried under my name."

"Why do you need that?" his words seemed clipped and short.

"Brian and I have run into a situation. I want you to know that the story is going public if you haven't already heard."

"What do you mean '*going public*'? You do realize that your records are classified!" his sputter shifted to angry.

"Jesus, you think I did this on purpose?" Trying to calm him, she explained, "I know that it's classified, but the band talked me into taking the empty spot, and it never occurred to me anyone would make a big deal about my being 'dead' until it happened. The show will be airing tonight if you want to watch and see what took place.

"I'm trying to figure out how to head this off. I'm really scared, Jim." He was the one person she knew would understand why, and she hung her head slightly, disappointed at her actions and the risk they faced.

"Yeah, well, you should be," he admonished, "Have you thought about completing your job?" His tone a touch frosty, Tori only breathed into the mouthpiece, unwilling to give him a knee-jerk response.

Inhaling for a deep sigh, she peered out of the bedroom window. The sun setting beautifully on the early December day, the sky held the promise of snow before Christmas. "I can't do that yet," she answered him calmly. "I need to try and work this out, see what comes of it."

"I understand," he replied in a calmer voice, "I'll get the records for you and let you know." He already had what she wanted, but chose to let her stew before he released the information to her.

"We're at the group house in New Jersey," she informed him quietly. "The sooner, the better." She gave him both the address and phone number and thanked him before she hung up the phone, hoping to hear from him later that night.

Heading back downstairs, Tori rejoined the others, who were chattering noisily until she entered the room. Glancing around at the silence, she inquired, "When can we expect Mark to get here?"

"He's on his way, sis," Brian assured her. "Don't worry, we'll set things straight if we can."

Eyeing the man she had beaten, she felt no sense of victory. They were in trouble, and fighting amongst themselves wasn't going to help. "What about your security guy, what's his name... Pete?"

"Oh, he called my cell while you were upstairs," Cody assured her. "He was sure pissed we left his ass at the studio, too. Said from now on, he'll decide when it's important enough to need his *personal* attention."

"Asshole," Michael intervened, "I think we need to consider looking for someone else. Someone who takes the role more seriously."

"What?" Collin laughed, "You want your old job back after all?"

"No," their former bodyguard replied flatly, "I want someone who's going to be responsible and diligent. A professional."

"He's diligent enough; he likes toys and gadgets, that's all. I think we're fine," Cody defended the man they had abandoned. "Besides, you're here, and I'm sure that makes him feel a little threatened. Ease up on him, and he'll do better."

Tori swung her gaze around the room, avoiding saying anything else. She had been working to boost her confidence in her decision to join the band, and nothing that had happened that day had helped her in that regard. The last thing she wanted was to make any more choices until they had discovered how bad the damage really had been.

Whatever Happens

Setting about making dinner, the group sent the housekeeper off to her quarters. Normally, they would allow her to prepare the meal, but having something to occupy their minds would prove useful.

Seeing his wife deep in thought, Michael inquired in German, "So, what did you find out?"

Quietly, she replied in kind, "I got ahold of Jim. He's going to track down what became of the other girl's body. The one they buried in my place."

Crinkling his nose as he listened to them, Cody asked in an irritated tone, "Why do you two do that? You always break off into some other language. Don't you think that's rude, when all of us wanna know what's going on?"

Tori cut her eyes over at her husband before she met the gaze of her accuser. She could tell he felt the stress of the situation, and felt a bit guilty that they had shut the group out by the alternate tongue. She repeated what she had learned in English, causing Cody's eyes to grow wide.

"Just like that, you called the FBI. Like it was no big deal." His mouth hung open slightly, obviously shocked at what she had been up to.

"Sorry. It's been a part of my life for so long, I really didn't give it much thought." Giving him a small grin, she recalled that there were still parts to her story she had not shared with them, and hoped she would never have to.

Sitting down to the meal, the group ate in relative silence. The food only half eaten, Mark Holt walked into the room, looking haggard. "Ok, what the hell is going on?" he wasted no time in getting to the point.

Not knowing what had been said to him, Tori could not fault the man for using what Collin had shared out of context. Giving him a nod, she indicated the empty seat at the table. Cleaning her fingers on her napkin, she started things off calmly, "What exactly has been put out, you know, into the public forum?"

He stared at her, ill at ease as he had been informed this had been a story that should never have been shared. Shifting into his chair, he spoke quietly, "Well, I told the crew for the show that you had been discovered, after having been believed to be dead for about twenty years."

Swallowing noticeably, he went on, "And, I told them you had been raised by men, so you weren't really what you might call a 'girly-girl.'" He gave her a weak grin, deciding to do some repair work on their relationship.

"Look, Tori; I realize you're a really smart girl. I've been thinking about what you did with the guitars, and it was a pretty neat trick. I guess I must have come across as a real asshole, and needed a quick lesson on manners. And, I didn't really understand anything about you, but I think I'm beginning to."

He stared at her, pausing for her to respond. She only blinked at him, so he continued, "Anyways, I really want things to go well for you and the rest of the guys. Whatever happens, I never meant to bring any harm to any of you."

Shifting her gaze to her plate, Tori folded her hands, giving herself a moment to think. After a full minute of reflection, she asked in a quiet voice, "Anyone else put anything more than that out there? Or is that the gist of what we have to worry about?" She lifted her chin to peer around the group, but no one spoke up.

"Alright then, I think we can handle this," she said as she slapped the table and grinned broadly.

Stunned, Brian demanded point blank, "So how're you gonna fix it? I mean, they know you were missing for twenty years, so I don't see how you're gonna hide that. The people you're afraid of will know what you're talking about."

Her eyes glistening, Tori shrugged, "Maybe they will," she admitted carefully, "Maybe they won't. I guess you could say, it's all a matter of perspective. I need to get the facts from the Feds, what they found out about the other girl. Then, I need to take control of the situation, and stop the flow of information. Everyone here understands nothing else leaves this room. Correct?"

The group cast glances at one another, wondering who among them would spill the beans. In the end, they agreed that no one else would share information about Tori, her past, or any other details about her life that they were not given explicit direction to share.

Her smile bright, Michael could see his wife had a plan, and laughed out loud, "Ok, baby girl, this I have to hear," leaning on elbows eagerly.

She shook her head slowly at her mate, aware that she had begun to like that he called her by her old nick-name. "I'm going back on the show. He wants to tell the world my story, and I'm going to give him the chance. We need to watch it tonight, see what they air. We'll call them tomorrow and offer them an exclusive interview, but it'll be on my terms."

"You think that'll work?" Collin asked doubtfully.

Tori turned her palm to the ceiling, "Why wouldn't it? You said it yourself; people eat this shit up. I tell them the parts I want them to know, and hopefully it won't be enough for anyone dangerous to connect the dots. The Feds have the truth locked down, and they aren't going to share anything about it, because it's all classified, like I said." She made a popping sound with her tongue, thinking about the Feds actually doing something useful for a change.

"That means the public will pretty much have to take me at my word," she continued, "All I have to do is convince them. Then, we go on about our business, go on the tour, or whatever we want to do. The danger is greater than it would have been, but in the end it was bound to happen. Someone would have eventually snooped out that particular part from Danny's past; I'm almost sure of it."

She paused to reflect on her plan for a moment. "I do have one request though, and I guess it's kind of a big one."

Collin answered eagerly, "Name it."

"I need two weeks off. The first two weeks of February. I have something personal I need to take care of." Her voice had dropped very low, and she eyed her husband, causing him to shift in his seat; he knew what she was talking about. Seeing their nods of agreement, Tori felt relieved that at least that portion of the future had been settled.

Continuing to discuss the particulars of the day's events, everyone agreed to allow the girl to take the lead on cleaning up the mess, and further swore to take her story to their grave. Giggling, she said softly, "I hope that won't be necessary, you know, anytime soon." Inhaling deeply, she released a heavy sigh, "Well, this has been exciting. If you'll excuse me, I think I'm ready for bed."

Michael followed her up the stairs, enjoying the view as they climbed, and watching her dark hair sway above her round rear end. Reaching their sanctuary, he shut the door behind them before allowing a loud gasp of air to spew from his tight lips. "You really think you can pull that off?"

Turning to lay her arms around his neck, she shook her dark curls, "I don't know, we'll see. I'll give it my best. You know I've gotten to be a pretty good actress at times."

He grinned, having seen how she could work people, especially men, when she wanted to. Placing his hands on her waist, he massaged her curves through the thin material of her tee. "And what about February; are you planning to go and have your treatment?"

Almost intuitively, she nodded, "I know this isn't the life you wanted to give our child. But I want to be ready if and when we decide to try. Besides, the doctor said if I were to become pregnant before the procedure had been completed, there might be a chance I would lose the baby and risk further injury to myself. I don't want that, either way."

Running his hands up and down her back, he had to agree, "That's good thinking, love. In case we were to have any accidents, which we both know can and does happen, at least we would be prepared." Leaning forward, he kissed his bride gently, "Have I told you lately that I love you?" he pushed his nose into her hair, nuzzling her ear.

Tori smiled, never doubting his devotion, "I love you, too." She drew him closer, "And I hope we have a long and happy, and perhaps much less exciting life together, in the years to come."

Michael chuckled at her sentiments, unable to disagree.

Stretching out on the bed, the couple snuggled while they watched the late night program, focusing on the details that were revealed, which weren't many. After seeing it, Tori beamed, aware that taking care of the near disaster might turn out easier than she had thought possible.

Like Old Times

Michael made sure to be up with his wife the following morning when she hit the gym. He had made a vow to himself while she was away taking care of the Scorpions that he would improve his physical condition, and he wanted to make up for what she had lost in order to regain her reproductive abilities. He loved the fact that she wanted to have his child, and believed she should feel free to do so without giving up part of her safety.

It seemed like old times to Tori, the two of them working side by side. His presence pushed her to work hard, even if she had backed off to almost half her training time, still being in excellent health. Raising her toes to the bar for her final rounds, she thought about his being there, pleased that he wanted to spend time with her and hoping it would continue as it inspired her deeply.

Back in their room, the couple indulged in a quick morning romp before their shower. After they were satisfied, they made themselves presentable and went down to breakfast. They had slept in until 9:00 am, but they were still the first ones up in the house, and Stella seemed pleased to make them a breakfast of scrambled eggs and bacon. Taking chairs on opposite sides of the same corner, the pair conversed quietly in German while they waited.

"So, I was thinking about the house," Michael spoke in a soothing tone. "After the tour, we should be able to spend some time back home and finish more of the repairs to it."

Tori felt a stab of guilt that they had left their small town and friends in such a rush. "You think they miss us?" her voice sounded small, having picked up on his calling the tiny town *home*.

Smiling, he confessed, "I've been keeping in touch with Trish. She's looking after our place, and collecting the rent from our tenant. I also arranged for her and Larry to retrieve your truck from the airport, and he's going to borrow it for a bit. The two of them seem quite cozy, by the way."

"Really?" she smiled, "I wondered when Trish would get her second chance after how things turned out with the boys' father. How are they taking it?"

Staring into space for a moment, he adjusted his grip on his cup and puckered his lips, "They miss us," he admitted. "But we'll be able to visit our young friends soon enough. We can't live two lives. This is where we are, and that's how it is. Besides, you know Steven is going to want to hear all about your adventures with the band, as taken as he is with music." His words brought a smile to her face, as she pictured the younger of the two, ten years old, and as feisty as ever.

Having their plates placed before them, the couple enjoyed the delicious meal, thanking the dark haired woman wholeheartedly. They were still eating when they were joined by Cody and Brian, who were eager to have some as well, and the conversation shifted in language and tone.

It occurred to her that Brian spoke French, as did she and Michael. "We should teach you and Collin how to speak it," she pointed out to Cody as he devoured his meal greedily.

He shrugged, "I don't really get the need for it."

"It gives us an edge," his new bandmate tried to explain. "When we're around other people, we have more of a chance of sharing conversations that are private, or more private."

"I see," he replied, considering the girl and her need for secrecy. Cody had to admit; Tori was not like anyone he had ever known. Even after hearing her story about being raised to fight and do horrific things, he had been surprised how easily she bested his buddy in the driveway. Considering her offer, he became slightly intrigued, "Would it be hard?"

Tori gave him a wide grin, "It's like anything else; it takes practice. If you want to play an instrument or learn a new song, you spend time with it."

With a small shrug, he agreed, "Sure, I guess if you're willing to teach me. What would it hurt?"

Tori smiled a little larger, "Then it's settled. I'll give you a few words each day to practice and build your vocabulary. And we'll go through some grammar lessons from time to time."

At that moment, the phone rang, and Stella held it out to Tori. Jumping up from her chair, she grasped the headset and made her way over to the wide window to peer into the back yard. "Hello?" she asked in an eager tone.

"Hello. I have news for you," said a male voice on the other end.

Tori smiled to hear Jim Godfry, prepared to divulge the information that she required. Clearing his throat, he read her the main parts of the report, "The girl's body was exhumed, and identified as that of the little girl we had anticipated. She had been abducted a short distance from the location of the burned out vehicle. Apparently, they had snatched her and placed her inside the car within a matter of hours. Her parents were glad to be finally able to lay her to rest, and they weren't informed as to how or where she was located. That seems to be the extent of it, sealed up nice and tight.

The connection between her and you are not public knowledge."

Hearing his words, she became excited at the prospect of keeping the rest of her story contained. "Thanks, Jim. I really appreciate the information." Hanging up the phone, she turned eagerly to her brother, "That settles it, how do we contact Mark?"

Pulling out his cell, he gave her the number. "You know," he said as she dialed the digits into the cordless device, "I seriously think we need to get you guys some mobile phones."

Tori shook her head, listening into the earpiece. *Someday I need to explain to him why those aren't a good idea.* Holding up her hand as their manager picked up the other end, she dove in directly, "Hey, Mark; this's Tori. Have you contacted the studio about my exclusive with Kyle?"

"Actually, I just hung up with them and was about to call you," he replied in a friendly tone. "I'm rather impressed at how easy it was to arrange. Kinda scares me a bit actually, almost as if they were expecting our call. Or at least pleased to get it."

"I'm sure they were," she laughed slightly. "So what's the deal, then?"

"We need to be at the studio at one pm for filming."

"Nice. We'll be there." Ending the call, the girl tossed out a quick briefing before heading up the stairs, and Brian went to wake Collin and have him up and ready to go as well.

The group's mood seemed surprisingly upbeat at the occasion when they regrouped to climb into the limo. The drummer a chatterbox, he pointed out the free publicity would do wonders for the group, which earned him a momentary cold stare, "Not that I will be doing anything like this again," he quickly recanted. He didn't really like the times she was upset, noticing that she ran hot and cold, mostly cold, and he remained grateful she had refrained from beating him in the face.

Although the men of the group began to appear a little anxious as the studio drew closer, the girl came across as calm as ever, at least from what they could see. Practiced at hiding her emotions, she kept her bundle of nerves hidden away behind her blank stare, her mind going over exactly what she wanted to say when the time came, and how far she would have to go to be convincing.

When they arrived, they were shown to the dressing room, and the young woman that fixed hair and makeup came in with a cheerful greeting. She finished quickly, and again, the group waited to be called, this time in near silence. The time ticked by, and they were led out, where the guys all took seats along the front row to watch, while Tori waited on the side of the stage.

Feeling a mild rush of adrenaline, causing her hands to tingle, she had the old familiar urge to have a drink. Instead, she asked if there might be some coffee to be had, and someone produced a large mug of the black steaming liquid for her. Holding it steady with both hands, Tori sipped the brew, relaxing into the persona that she would be presenting in front of the camera.

A short time later, the announcement came, and she walked across the hard wood floor, poised and ready for the show. Having a look around, the lights seemed too bright, and she could not see out in the audience, but she knew they were there because she could hear the polite applause; the crowd seemed a little unimpressed with the show's guest.

Reaching her chair, she held her hand out and permitted him to take her fingers, and then drew it back, her features remaining expressionless as if made of fine porcelain.

The first thing out of his mouth was, "So, how tall are

you?" This brought a hint of a grin to her face, as if she got that a lot.

"I'm just over six foot," she replied in a tiny voice, shifting into her chair.

"Uh-huh," he made small talk for another minute, "And how long have you been playing the guitar?"

Giving her typical short response, "Acoustic for years, electric only about a year and a half."

Kyle nodded, stroking his chin, looking as if he were getting ready to pounce. "And you are of course Brian Madson's sister, correct?"

Tori felt as if she were watching a snake coil, ready to strike as he toyed with his prey. Giving him a wide-eyed stare, she agreed that they were siblings with a small nod.

"Even though his sister died, along with their parents, some twenty years ago," he leaned away from her, his expression challenging her to deny his words.

Nodding, she agreed, "Yeah… Yeah, that's right. I was dead twenty years. Had my own little gravestone and everything." Tracing the outline of a small monument in the air with her index fingers, she gave him another faint smile.

Licking his lips, he appeared at a loss for words and rubbed his chin again as he had expected the accusation to lead somewhere explosive.

"You know," he snapped lightly, "You can elaborate anytime you want to explain things. I mean, if she had been found alive, we would have heard about it. So, why haven't we?" He nodded at her, beginning to feel uneasy about her manner.

Tori only bobbed her head as well, her crystal blue eyes fixed on him, boring into him, almost glazed.

His tongue skimming his upper lip, he continued, "You don't have anything else to say?"

She shrugged, and gave another small reply, "Like what?

People thought I was dead, and I wasn't. I don't know why you haven't heard," she denied flatly.

"So, where were you?" he demanded, a bit of irritation in his voice.

Her eyes grew even wider, and she looked timid as her voice seemed to grow unsteady, "I was taken." She watched his jaw drop, pausing for effect, "A man took me, after the car wrecked. I was barely five, and he kept me."

She stood and allowed her jacket to slide down her arms, swinging her long tresses out of the way to expose the marks on her left arm, the puckered burn on her bicep clearly visible. "The police thought I had burned up in the car, and they gave me a grave. It was an accident that I was found... saved."

Mouth hanging open, Kyle looked stunned, "Jesus, he did that to you?" He wanted a good story, but had not expected this. Staring at the girl who towered above him, she nodded her confirmation with a slight pout on her lips. "Wow," he stammered, "I'm curious why you agreed to come on the show." He had clearly become uncomfortable with the girl and her marked flesh.

Tori showed him her full set of perfect white teeth before allowing it to fade. Taking up her perch on the upholstered chair, she reeled him in, "I had to come. I live in a small town, and I never told anyone there what happened to me. I discovered firsthand what people can do when they are left to make up whatever story they want."

She paused, allowing him to think about those words for a moment, and then finished the thought, her features becoming overly expressive, conveying the deep emotion behind her words, "It was important that I come and tell the truth. It hurts for people to know, but it's less than the cruel things that would be said otherwise."

Eyes locked, he began losing confidence that he would

come off as a hero, exposing their secrecy and lies to the world. She did not appear to be deceitful, and he could see the pain in her crystal blue orbs. "How long since you got away from your captor?" he no longer asked his scripted questions, as they had taken a path he had not anticipated.

Tori swallowed hard, giving her typical pause and casting her eyes into the lights that hid the audience beyond. *How long had it been since the farmhouse in Iowa?* She quickly added the time.

"It's been about two years," she spoke breathlessly, exaggerating the span a bit. "It took them a while to locate my brother because I had been believed to be dead, and our parents are gone. They didn't even know who I was until they found him."

She had her jacket draped across her knees and toyed with the collar in a nervous fashion, causing the muscles beneath the lines on her arm to ripple. Kyle watched them, imagining how she must have suffered at the strange man's hand.

"Are you safe now?" his voice faltered, realizing they may have opened her to danger by bringing her in front of the camera.

Staring at him, her eyes melting into soft pools of grey, she nodded for a moment, then shrugged slightly to agree, "I'm ok. I'm not afraid of the man who abused me. He's gone now," she confessed with the slightest of grins.

Swimming in regret, he thanked her for coming on the show. "You are very brave to share your past with us." He smiled, but did not feel happy, and wanted to talk about something else with his guest.

"So," he shifted gears, "You actually play very well. I was pretty impressed with the new makeup of the band." He nodded at her, wanting to make amends for his harsh attitude towards her. "Collin on the drums and Brian on the bass seems to work well. How do you feel about playing with them?"

Tori's thin grin curled her lips further. Tilting her head slightly, her face stunningly beautiful, she cooed, "Oh, I love to play. It's the one thing that makes me feel right."

She paused, and his smile reached his eyes, feeling happy their new topic pleased her, and she gave him more, "I was really anxious about it at first, but they convinced me that I was the one they wanted."

Tori shook her long dark curls, playing him as well as she did a set of strings. They chatted for several more minutes before he dismissed her, smiling at her genuinely and glad they had come to friendly terms.

Arriving back in her dressing room alone, she exhaled a deep breath to cleanse the excitement from her blood. The guys joined her shortly, and Mark informed her that Kyle wanted to speak with her after the taping, if she didn't mind waiting.

Taking a seat in front of the wide mirror, she sat quietly, hands on her lap. Michael made his way over to give her a small kiss, stroking her hair and trying to read her mood. She smiled meekly at him and reached up to lightly caress his jaw to relax his clenched muscles. She could see the worry in his honey brown eyes, but she knew the show had been the worst part, and it would all be downhill from there.

A short time later, a knock at the door announced Kyle's arrival, and grinning ear to ear, he let himself in. Reaching out to her, he shook her hand vigorously and thanked her once again for coming. "I know this wasn't easy for you, and I hope that it'll help put some of the questions about your life and your past to rest."

Tori nodded, her blue eyes sparkling, and she continued to work her magic over him.

"You're really a quiet person," he laughed, "Not like so

many of the people who come through here. You'll have to keep in touch, let me know how things are going or if there's ever anything we can do for you here on the show. We wouldn't mind helping out if we can." He had held onto her hand after the shake and released it as he finished speaking as if to indicate she could now go.

Smiling at the rest of the band members, he gave them a small wave and bade them farewell. One of the staffers showed the group out through a different hallway, and so there were no reporters to torment them this time, an indication that she had gained a good deal of respect during her time on stage that day. Climbing into the long black car, she finally sighed in relief that it was over.

Jingle Bells

After going public with their big news, the tension level in the house seemed to drop dramatically, with everyone getting along amiably. With only three weeks until Christmas, the group decided to take a shopping trip to buy presents. Together, they piled into the limo and headed to Broadway to make a day of it.

Tori loved the Levi's shop the best and picked out a variety of new items to add to her wardrobe. She also purchased some gifts for her husband and her brother, noticing that everyone had a large number of bags stuffed with wrapped packages by the end of the afternoon. Settling into the ride home, she jokingly announced, "I guess being 'famous' isn't that unusual after all. No one hardly gave us a second glance."

"Haha, this wasn't an outing to judge from," her brother teased, "We didn't attract a lot of attention, for the most part, and only ran into a few fans that recognized us. It comes and goes, and you learn to enjoy the calmness when you can, because it doesn't last. There are reporters and crowds, potentially, everywhere."

Michael nodded nervously at her, "You may be in for a real shock at how crazy it can get, especially when you become more of a familiar face."

Tori only eyed the two of them with a tiny grin, unsure if she really believed either of them or not.

When they arrived at the house and cleared the gate, Brian announced in his playful manner, "I got a surprise for you, sis."

"What kind of surprise?" she peered at his bundles, assuming that some of the boxes were for her.

"Nah, it's already in the house," the grin spreading across his face, his pleasure obvious, he indicated with an extended finger.

Exiting the car, she caught her breath, able to see the massive collage of color and lights through the panes of glass. The group hurried inside to take in the floor to ceiling Christmas tree that stood in the front window in the living area off to the left of the foyer.

Michael felt a small stab of jealousy, peering up at the enormous decoration, it obviously being much more spectacular than the tiny one the couple had shared a year prior. "Wow, that's a hell of a tree," he mumbled, staring at the ornament laden branches.

Taking his hand, Tori reassured him, "You know, love; the guitar you gave me last year will always be the best present ever." Somehow, he doubted that.

After a group dinner, the couple said their good nights and made their way to their room for a quiet evening. The rest of the household geared up for a party, as there seemed to be one every night to some degree, and the two of them were becoming well practiced at avoiding them.

Inside their chamber, Michael made his way over to the window, watching the light snow outside that had begun to fall. Reaching up to catch her hands when she slid them around from behind, he held them pressed against his chest for a moment.

Tori could sense his preoccupation, and she waited patiently for him to open up.

Sighing deeply, he spoke in a low tone. "I want you to know; I really do support your choice to be here and to play with the band."

"Thank you, love. Your being with me means a lot." She had stiffened at his words, afraid of what might be coming next.

Massaging the back of her hand, he conceded, "I've been doing some thinking, and after what happened at the studio, I'm really not sure I can go on the road with you for the tour. Not like we had planned."

Tori stood stunned. "What do you mean you can't go?" she stammered. "I thought you were going to be there with me, by my side, and all that." Her words strained, she tried desperately not to raise her voice at him.

Gripping her hand tightly, he tried to explain. "At the studio, I realized, I want to take care of you. I want to look after you, and that means that I would be like your personal bodyguard. But, if that's the role I'm taking, then I can't be your husband."

She could hear the conflict within him, which added to her confusion. Gripping his shoulder, she forced him to turn around to face her, angry and demanding, "That doesn't make sense, Michael. Is this because of the differences you have with Peter Farside? Or are you really afraid we're going to be found?"

"No, it doesn't have anything to do with him. Not really." Inhaling slowly, he tried again, "And no, I'm not afraid of being found. I just can't look after you the way you need to be from where I am. I can't look after you the way that I want to, from where I am. I'm too close to you. I can be your husband and your lover, or I can be your security, but I can't do both."

"So you don't think we're safe," she stood up straighter, not buying his reasons, "Even though you claim that we are."

"I didn't say that," he reached for her hair, "I just know that if I need to see something, if I need to act, I don't know that it will happen if I'm not in the right frame of mind. I'm sorry. I can't ride on your bus with you." He heaved a deep sigh, "You distract me too much, and I think that'll be the only way to solve the problem. I can't let anything happen to you."

Searching his eyes, she wasn't sure what to say. Finally, she conceded, "I want you to go. If you can't be on the bus with us, then ride with the security team and keep your distance. If that's what it takes for you to feel right about this, then I'm ok with that. I need you there." The thought made her wince, as that had been the role Henry played for so many years, watching from afar; but at least he would be close.

Pursing his lips, he nodded slightly, "I'm considering doing that, but I won't promise anything. We'll see how things go between now and then before I make up my mind."

Leaning her forehead against his, the pair stood and swayed left and right, the white puffs drifting to the ground visible through the window beside them. Exhaling noisily, he indicated the wide frame, "Remember the last snowfall we shared?"

Tori smiled, recalling the surprise snow day back in Texas, and nodded, "The day we met Trish's boys. They walked into our lives and never left." She could feel his sadness, and it occurred to her that he might be homesick.

"Do you wanna go home? I mean, go home for Christmas?" she asked meekly, considering how it might improve his outlook.

Shaking his head, he refused. "Your brother expects us to stay here and share the holiday with him, and we should. It'll be our first family Christmas since you found him. It's only right," Michael tried to sound understanding, even if he didn't completely feel that way.

Kissing him, Tori sent her fingers gliding across his wide chest and around his shoulders, feeling the warmth of his hardened muscles through his tee. She had come into the room with the intention of making love, but felt drained by the sad tidings he had given her. Renewed ambition set over her, and she pushed forward decisively, placing her mouth over his and preventing him from speaking further.

Pulling at his clothes, she lifted his shirt over his head and tossed it on the chair next to them. Using her tongue, she wet his nipple through his mat of curly hair and ran her fingers across it playfully. Her touch excited him, and he splayed his digits lightly across her waist, searching for the hem of her shirt to remove it.

Emitting a small giggle, Tori took a step back and began to remove her own clothing, not stopping until she had fully undressed and her long black hair fell around her naked curves. Her lips curled in a soft smile, her eyes full of tenderness, she pulled at his button and zipper, and the remainder of his garments fell to the floor.

Lifting her chin towards him, she backed to the bed and perched on the edge of it. He made his way up to her, stopping in the perfect position for her to reach out and toy with him before taking him into her mouth.

Tori had always loved how much he excited her, and she him, her fingers grasping eagerly as she pulled and teased.

Michael enjoyed her playfulness, caressing her scalp and running his digits through her dark tresses while she fondled him. He allowed her to do so for several minutes before removing himself from her grasp and dropping to his knees before her.

Tugging at her legs to spread them wide, he laid her back

on the edge of the bed so that he could reach her easily with his face and fingers, exploring her soft folds beneath her trimmed mat of fur, almost as if he were opening a fragile gift. She moaned slightly, her hands anxiously moving back and forth between his brown waves and her own flesh that demanded the attention of her trembling fingers.

His need urging him for more, he stood and indicated for her to move to the center of the bed. Grappling with her legs while he faced her, he pushed them down, folding them so that her ears and knees were almost connected, claiming her in a swift driving motion that took her breath away. He moved against her with heavy thrusts, and she panted into them, relishing his forcefulness, the wetness oozing down to coat her forbidden crinkles of flesh.

The two were as noisy as ever with their grunts and groans, lost in the animalistic roots of their desire. Eventually freeing her legs, she wrapped their silky smoothness around him, squeezing him slightly as he leaned over to kiss her, and then lick and bite at the tender skin that covered her neck. Clawing at his shoulders and hair, she begged him for more, and then lifted her feet towards the roof to allow him to punish her more fully.

Giving in to her demands, he sat up and rolled her over onto her face, so that her rear end stuck up into the air and made his way inside of her. Tori loved it when he drove her in this manner, crying out sharply at his eager stabs. As she cried for more, he tried to appease her with hard, almost violent strokes that caused him to pant, the sweat dripping from his sticky flesh. He grasped at the roundness of her hips, using them for leverage as he worked, Tori hanging on to the blankets that covered their bed in a mixture of pain and lust.

After a few minutes, he teased her with his thumb, rubbing the folds of her round orifice, tickling the tender flesh and allowing her to become lost in their actions more fully before she had finished. Knowing her trembling signal, he squeezed her ribs as he released, her breathing in deep gasps as her insides undulated in waves of pleasure, her grasp weakened to nothing as she clung to the cloth.

Their desire spent, the couple dropped down onto the flat surface, their bodies still intertwined. His arm looped around beneath her, Michael's hand became buried inside her thick curls that allowed her skin to hide and peek at him in small sections. He pulled gently at her locks as she tantalized him, and he felt the strength of their bond weighing heavily in his chest. He loved her so much, he almost felt trapped by his devotion.

Lying still, wrapped in the warmth of their greedy sex, the couple could hear the sound of Jingle Bells emanating from somewhere in the house. Humming softly to the melody, Michael ran his fingers over the red marks that were visible where he had held on to her too tightly a few moments before, only feeling slightly guilty as it had also pleased her that he had done so. Eventually, they moved to the shower, continuing to share kisses and to express their fondness for one another in kind, each knowing they had done their best to satisfy the other.

Nobody's Angel

Things continued to run fairly smoothly in the house as Michael and Tori made the effort to avoid the rowdier activities of the other three. Eventually, this got old for the girl, and on the last night before Cody and Collin were to leave for Nebraska, she decided she wanted to be a part of the crowd.

"What do you mean you're going downstairs?" Michael grabbed her arm, swinging her around to face him, "You're going to join the party?"

"Yeah, I'm going to join the party," she stated flatly, her eyes dropping to his lips as her hand wafted around to indicate their prison, "I'm tired of hiding up here like a hermit. Besides, it sounds like fun."

Her husband clenched his jaw, his hand gripping her arm more firmly than he intended before she wrenched it away from him. "You got a problem with that?" she demanded crisply, her eyes darting back up to meet his, aware that he really didn't like it, but unable to give in to him at the moment.

"No," he dropped the word calmly, "No problem. Let me change, and I'll go with you," he tried to buy some time.

"Don't be silly," she laughed out loud, "It's our house, we can go buck naked if we want to." His brow shot up at the comment, not even doubting that she was serious, and she continued, "I'm going. Come and find me if you have to change. Or, whatever."

Giving herself a quick glance in the mirror, Tori closed the door behind her, aware that he hadn't moved and stood, staring after her in disbelief. Her fingers trailing the banister, she descended the front staircase, and found her way into the living area that held the massive tree.

Pushing her way through the bottleneck and into the room, she looked around at the groups that were strewn about, many of them drunk or high. Two couples shared the couch, both missing important pieces of clothing, and she found herself staring at them in surprise, as she had experienced scenes of that nature too many times to count in her previous life.

Only staying for a moment, she retraced her steps, taking the narrow hall that wound through the center of the house and came out in the kitchen on the back side. The constant thud of the music beginning to make her innards spasm, she forced her countenance into a pleasant shape to mask the few unpleasant memories that bombarded her.

Entering the oversized room, the stench of alcohol greeted her, and her mouth began to water. Smiling as she gazed around the wide expanse, she moved up next to the table, where several shot glasses and bottles of liquor were scattered across it, obviously a large quarters match in full swing .

Her brother sat on one end, shirt off, with a small blond rubbing his smooth chest from behind. "Hey, sis," he blurted too loudly, "Wanna join us? Make some room, guys," he demanded before she had even responded.

"No, Danny; it's ok," she held her palms up in a stopping motion, as a pair of hands slid around her waist, and a warm breath caressed her ear.

"Hey, beautiful," the male voice cooed, his fingers moving across her flat belly in a circular motion before pulling her tightly against him, causing his exaggerated bulge to press against her rear end. "Let's go someplace private," he continued as the digits found a nipple, her heart doubling in speed at the excitement the intimate action produced.

Catching his hand, Tori slipped slightly to the side, but not completely out of his grasp, "Collin, honey; you're drunk," her voice tinkling lightly as she spoke.

"I know," he laughed himself, pushing her back against the wall next to them, caging her between his arms, "But you can't tell me you're not tempted. I see the way you look at me, you know."

Tori's mouth hung open, a small smile refusing to be wiped away, "How I look at you? Are you kidding me? That's so lame," she laughed out loud, and he leaned forward, placing his lips over hers.

Her hands pushed against his bare chest, only half resisting his advances. She could feel the pulse in her neck, her panties already growing moist at the thought of being in such a compromising position.

When he ended the kiss, he kept his face close to hers, his lips on her cheek, "So whatdaya say? Share and share alike?"

His reference startled her, and images of lying across the table while a group of men took their turns at her sprang into her mind. Her smile fading, she licked her upper lip, "No, Collin; not tonight. Ok? I just wanna hang out for a while. Listen to the music and… mingle."

"Suit yourself," he pulled his arms down and stumbled away from her.

The air surrounding her felt colder with the removal of his presence, and she shivered, feeling a surprising stab of sadness to see him go.

Straightening herself and smoothing her clothing, she made her way over to the fridge, where she retrieved a bottle of water, only to be manhandled briefly by a second man, who she had never met before. This time, Michael intervened, removing the unwanted hand from her waist and telling him to get lost.

"Wow, I wasn't sure you were going to show," she teased him as she pulled out a second bottle to hand her mate, noting that he had, in fact, not changed clothes. Realizing he may have seen the display, she only felt slightly guilty at the encounter with Collin. Lifting her chin, she waited for him to respond as his brown eyes bore into her.

Without speaking, Michael reached and grasped her hand, jaw set as he led her through the far door and down the passage that came out at the lounge, which held a bar and pool table. Guiding her inside, he indicated that she should choose a cue, and he ran the couple lying across the green felt off to another part of the house, with a booming, "Hey, guys; get a room!"

Giggling at the way he acted, Tori continued to smile as she selected a maple shaft and watched her husband place the balls into the rack for a simple game of eight ball. "You any good?" she inquired.

"Does it matter?" he tossed back, unable to suppress a grin of his own. *Damn she's gorgeous. I'm gonna kick the shit out of that man if he ever touches her again.* He sneered as he recalled what he had seen before Collin had been dispensed. "What shall we play for?"

Her smile shriveled into an evil grin, knowing the thing she would want from him he would never do, whether he won the right or not. But what if she won it? Staring at him, her mind turned as she wanted to be careful how she worded her request.

Opening the bottle of water, she took a long drink, and

placed it on the table in the corner. Her back turned, she peered over her shoulder at him, her long black mane hanging behind her.

"Oh, you know, we don't really have to wager anything, do we?" she spun the phrase coyly, and he smiled, leaning on the table with straight arms.

"Well, if you're going to have guys feeling you up in the kitchen, I figure I might as well have my shot, right love?"

The smile disappeared from her lips, aware that he had seen everything that had taken place. Turning to face him squarely, she could feel her nerve slipping away, "He cornered me," she defended, "I wasn't there on purpose."

"Yeah," he breathed, "And I could see how hard it was to get away from him, too. Choose the wager. Whatever it is that you want most. Then I'll tell you mine."

Tori ran her finger along the side of the table, moving slowly around to the far side while keeping her eyes fixed on him, curious what he would ask for. "Maybe we should just put up money. Like, twenty a game or something."

He laughed again, "That's chicken shit, baby girl. You wanted to come down here, to enjoy the *party*. Make a real wager."

She didn't like the way the word *party* rolled off his lips, and she stopped moving. "Alright, we make it for the night. If I win…" her voice trailed away, a little afraid to actually ask him for it, "If I win, we make it dirty. Really dirty."

He shook his head with a chuckle, "Is that the best you can do? I know what you mean, but you can't even say it? A badass bitch such as yourself?" He had been giving her a twisted grin, enjoying tormenting her, but something about the hurt expression that crossed her face stopped him cold. "I'm sorry; I didn't mean it like that."

She looked down at his chest, the table still between them, "Yeah well, that's the best that I can do," and she blinked rapidly for a moment. "What's yours?" her voice shook slightly as she demanded to hear his terms.

"We go home," he stated bluntly. "If I win more games than you, after the tour is over, we go home."

Tori stared at him, air caught in her chest; "That's it? We already agreed we were going home anyways. That's a stupid wager, Michael," her voice went up as she rebuked him, angry that she had made a real request, and he had blown her off.

"I mean for good."

Jaw dropped, she coughed; "What? You're kidding me. Are you asking me to quit the band? You're the one who convinced me to be here, God damn it!"

Reaching over, he picked up the cue ball, holding it in his hand as he pointed his index finger at her, "No. I said you should choose what you want to do and not because you were afraid. In the end, it was your choice. I wanted to take you home. I still do." His voice dropped as he spun the ball in his palm, "It's the thing that I want most."

She blinked at him for a moment, "I don't want to play."

"What do you mean you don't wanna play?" he waved his arms around. "It's just a bet! Haven't you ever gambled before?"

"Are you going to give me what I want if I win?"

He squeezed the ball, as if it would compress in his firm grip, rolling his tongue around as he considered the question. After a lengthy pause, he nodded, "Yeah, if you win more games than me, I'll give you what you want."

"How many times?" she demanded, lifting her chin.

He burst out laughing, "What the hell kind of question is that?"

"A legitimate one," she countered evenly. "If you win, you get something that's forever. I want the same. If I win, you give me what I want... from now on."

Michael stared at her for a moment, then rolled the ball across the table to her with a nod, "You're one hell of a horse trader, ya know that? Sure, as often as you like, I will treat you like a filthy whore. Your break."

Ignoring the jab, Tori placed the cue ball behind the imaginary line and chalked her cue. After a few practice strokes, she sent it crashing into the cluster of balls, two of them falling into a pocket, one of them the cue ball. "Fuck!" she swore loudly.

Michael laughed, retrieving the white sphere. "Hmmm, tough break," he snickered at his pun and proceeded to run the table. Calling the final shot, he sank the eight and returned his stick to the rack, "Thanks for the game."

Turning, he could hear her calling after him as he made for the door, "Wait a minute, that wasn't fair! You cheated; God damn it!"

Swinging around, he faced her squarely, "I cheated? I don't see how... the wager was, that if I won more games than you, I won the bet." She had made her way up behind him and stood toe to toe with him, his eyes only slightly higher than her own as she narrowed them at him. "You never specified how many games," he finished in a quieter tone.

Fuck me, I didn't. Son of a bitch. She had been so eager at the thought of trapping him into giving in to her, she had missed that part of the deal. "I assumed it would be more than one."

"Well, you know what happens when we assume things," he teased her with a small grin, his hand catching hers to play with her fingers. "You remember that song of yours, Nobody's Angel?"

"Yeah, what about it?" she demanded, still pissed that he had gotten the better of her.

"I always think about that song. I wonder if it's true, if

you really are that cold-hearted on the inside. I guess come summer, we'll find out if it is," he squeezed her palm before releasing it.

Catching her breath, "What's that supposed to mean?" her blue eyes sparked angrily.

Shoving his hands in his pockets he grinned, "It means, that's when we find out if you'll keep your word." Leaning forward, he kissed her gently, brushing her cheek with his nose, his heart pounding in his chest. Stepping back, he turned and left her there, heading for the stairs to make his way to bed.

Like It or Lump It

Tori could feel the anger boiling inside her as she watched his back disappear. *Son of a bitch*, she continued to curse him under her breath. *That was low,* but in the end she knew it had been her own fault. *Bastard.*

Strolling over to the bar, she found the access and made her way around behind it, where a seemingly endless supply of bottles stood in a row. Making her way down, she ran her finger lightly across the labels, stopping to pull her hand away as if it had been burned when she came to the right one. Staring at it for a moment, she licked her upper lip, her heart continuing to knock against her ribs.

Her fingers trembling slightly, she reached out to grasp the slender neck, pulling it against her chest and cradling it there while she searched for a glass. Finding one, she sat it on the bar, pouring the shot and placing the container on the wooden top with a loud thud.

Breathing in shallow pants, Tori sang along with the music that filtered in from somewhere else in the house. Her tongue slid over her lip again, and she rocked her head side to side, seeming to stretch her neck while she considered the burn that would follow the lifting of the tumbler. Reaching out with a single finger, she skimmed it lightly around the edge, picturing it being placed against her mouth as she drank.

What the hell are you waiting for? She stared at the glass. *Michael won't like me doing this.* Her finger trembled as she swiped the edge again. *Of course, if he doesn't like it, he can lump it.* The thought made her smile for a moment, easing her anger at her mate. *That was a pretty good prank, really. I never saw it coming.* She had never thought of her husband as smart before.

But that was a good move. All he had to do was play until he had the lead and then quit. She smiled at the idea that he had beaten her. *Maybe we're more evenly matched than I realized.*

"Ya gonna drink that?"

Tori jumped visibly and swung her gaze towards the voice to find a short kid standing next to her. "What?"

"ARE YOU GONNA DRINK THAT!?!" he shouted, pointing at the glass that sat in front of her.

Looking at the small container as if it might bite her, Tori drew her hand away from the beverage and slowly backed away from the bar.

"No. You can have it." Without waiting for his response, she darted out of the room and made her way up the stairs, realizing before she got to the top that she couldn't go back to their room. *It's too soon;* she rationalized, *and if I do, then it's like he wins... again. I can't let that happen.*

Moving quietly down the hall, Tori opened the door to the bedroom next to theirs and peeked inside, half expecting to find people in it as the house crawled with party guests. Finding the space unoccupied, she closed the door and locked it, not wanting to be disturbed.

Flicking the light on, she could see that it had been lain out the same as theirs. Deciding she liked it better dark, she turned the light off and made her way down between the bed and the bathroom wall, putting her shoulder into the corner and resting her forehead against the print of the paper covering. Her mind still turning, she recalled the last time she had slept in a corner.

Thanksgiving Day, or the day after really. The day Michael told her she had to join the band. *He denied it tonight, but I know he said it that way.* She exhaled loudly in disgust. *And he made that bet, so I'm supposed to go home with him after the tour and quit the band.* She cursed him all over again while she drifted off to sleep.

Tori awoke sometime later to blinding white light. Using her hand to cover her eyes, she screamed out, "What the fuck?!?" barely able to make out the outline of her husband standing over her.

Michael panted slightly, trying to slow his breathing. The house had gone quiet hours ago, and he had waited patiently for a while, before he had gotten worried and begun his search. "You ok?" he asked as he wiped his mouth with his arm, trying to appear calm.

"Yeah, I'm fine, could you turn the fucking light off?" she demanded crossly.

Hopping towards the switch, he snapped it crisply, "Sorry." Pausing, he drew a cleansing breath, relieved that she had been in the room, instead of someone else, after he went to the trouble to pry the lock. *And she's alone.* He hated to admit that part had concerned him the most.

Using the wall as his guide, he made his way back around and sank down next to her on the floor. "You gave me quite a scare," he admitted softly. "Thought something might have happened to you."

"Nope. I'm fine. Just pissed, that's all."

"Cause you lost our bet, huh," he stated with a small degree of satisfaction.

"Yup. Course, I can see that you would've felt the same way if it had been you having to pay up." She smiled at the thought of him bending her over and using the gel, the way everyone else always did. *Well, almost everyone else.*

"There's no way I was going to lose," he stated confidently.

"Yeah, I figured that out after you left." She sounded a little sad, and he looked over at her sideways, able to make out her silhouette in the dim light.

"I was really surprised you didn't see it before."

"Nope. I'm not that smart, I guess," she wafted her hand, as if she were shooing a fly away from her face.

"Sure you are. Smartest girl I ever met. Maybe the smartest person. Just didn't have your head in the game at the moment, so to speak." He grinned, "You don't have to honor the wager if you don't want to."

Tori cut her eyes over at him, "If I don't have to honor it, then what was all that bullshit about my song, and finding out if I'm really a cold hearted bitch. I told you I am. I have no intention of giving up on the band. Whether you like it or not, I'm here, and I'm not going to quit."

Michael dusted at his pant leg nervously, "Yeah, I know. And I don't really want you to quit. Not for me. If you quit, I want it to be because that's what you want to do, ya know?"

She could see his teeth gleaming as he grinned. "You mean that?" she asked calmly, feeling herself being drawn to him.

"Of course. I always want what's best for you. I want you to make good choices and to have a good life. A happy life. I can't give you everything, but I'll give you everything that I can," he said cryptically.

She nodded, glad she had left the glass sitting on the bar. "I really do love you, Michael Anderson," she said calmly, causing him to laugh.

"Yeah, some days I'm sure you do. And I love you, too," his voice trailed away as he spoke. He reached for her in the darkness, ready to take her back to their room, where there would be no chance of being interrupted while he showed her how much.

Safe and Secure

The next morning, three days before Christmas, Tori took an early run. As her off day, it would be all the workout she allowed herself. Michael headed to the gym, and she snuck in before he had finished to observe him as he worked. She loved how hard he worked, and enjoyed taking in the show, keenly aware that he pushed himself much harder than he had in the past. His skin glistening with sweat, he reached for a towel when he finished, causing her mind to go blank for a moment, and her face to flush.

"What?" he demanded playfully.

"Nothing," she shook her head, "You look pretty good for an old guy," she grinned as she teased.

"Ha! I'm not old, baby girl. Older than you, but still young enough to take care of business," he winked at her and left what kind of business to her imagination.

Standing to accompany him out of the room, her smile faded, "Are you sure we're not in danger?" She could see the disappointment cross his face that they were back on that topic again, but she couldn't ignore her questions any longer.

"Naw, I told you not to be afraid, didn't I?" he laid the towel across his neck, in a twisted roll, guiding her to the stairs, "We're fine, love."

"Well, I've been thinking," she broached the subject cautiously, "About Peter Farside. Do you really think things are secure enough around here? And what about when we go out in public?" She paused at the door of their bedroom, "I've never been in this kind of position before, so I don't know if things are really good enough or not. I hate to say that if I wanted to break in, it would be a piece of cake. At least I'm pretty confident that it would be."

Taking her arm, he guided her into their bedroom, "I've kind of been wondering the same thing," he admitted quietly. "I tried to make suggestions, but he doesn't want to hear them, and the guys don't want to talk about replacing him, so that means we're pretty much stuck. You're still afraid I won't go on the tour, aren't you."

"Yeah," she admitted in a modest tone, "That's part of it I guess. You know, living with you, and the halfway house before that, are my only experiences at indoor life. I want to know that we're safe here. Maybe we could snoop around and see if things are up to snuff," she suggested, pretty confident that they weren't.

"Would it make you feel better if we did?" he pulled off his shorts and stood naked before her, ready to get in the shower.

Tori's eyes dropped, her voice growing faint, "Sure, we could do… that…"

He could tell she had lost her train of thought, grinning as he reached for her. "Ok, we'll do some snooping," he nuzzled her neck, his fingers gliding across her silky spandex, "Let's start here," he mocked, pushing his hand down her pants, searching for folds of flesh.

Tori giggled, her fingers gliding across his smooth muscles. "You're so bad," she whispered. "A little more so and you'd be perfect." Pressing her body against his, the pair spent the better part of the next hour doing the nasty things that made each other happy.

After they were showered and dressed, the couple made their way down for breakfast and to decide where to start their search. Enjoying their meal along with the others, the couple noticed that the rest of the group was busy making their own plans. Taking seats next to each other at their usual corner of the table, they would be able to have at least some privacy.

Tori used their German while she recalled what he had told her previously about the security of the estate. They had first discussed it when they had visited with Eli Founder, after the Scorpions had trashed the place. "You once had four guys, right? Gate, cameras, and two for patrolling?"

"That's right," he confirmed in kind. "But I know for a fact that all of those guys have been eliminated. There isn't really a team anymore, and Pete's pretty much it."

Her jaw dropped at hearing this, "You're kidding me. No one even guards the entrance?" They had come in and out a few times in the limo, but she had never noticed that there wasn't an actual person in the gatehouse.

"Nope, it's electronic. Same with the cameras. No one watches the monitors anymore; it's all computerized. Anything out of the ordinary sets off an alarm on his phone, and he takes care of it." Michael grimaced as he described what he had learned about the new system.

"You already checked it all out then. Even before I asked," she eyed him warily.

Turning his palm to the ceiling, he shrugged, "Well, yeah, I guess I did, more or less. I wanted to be sure. Like you." He smiled, hoping she didn't lose confidence over the issue.

Finishing the meal, Tori felt eager to have a look at the set up for herself. Listening to the others before she left the table, she recalled that Cody and Collin were leaving later that day for Nebraska. "So, when're you guys coming back?"

"We'll be back New Year's Eve day," Cody supplied, "We got a big bash planned that night."

Tori giggled, "Another one?" She grimaced, recalling how her one and only attendance had worked out for her, "You guys party a lot, you know that."

"We're rock stars, what did you expect?" Collin shrugged at her, seemingly unaware of their moment against the wall the night before. "Livin' the dream, babe."

Staring at him with a slack jaw, she decided not to bring it to his attention. "Well, you guys have fun, and we'll see you in a week," she smiled, thinking that the oversized dwelling would be a little lonely without everyone there.

Leaving the guys to be on their way, Tori followed Michael through the house while he gave her the particulars on where the alarms and triggers were located. She felt disgusted to find that none of the second-floor windows were wired. "So, what if someone climbs up?"

"First, they have to get onto the estate. Then, they would have to make it up to the house without being detected, which wouldn't be easy. Plus, the climb to even get there would be difficult and or hazardous. It would take a special person to accomplish all that. I have to admit, I'm not real concerned about it," he tried to soothe her troubled thoughts.

Making their way out to the gate, Tori peered into the vacant guard's booth, noticing that it had been shuttered in such a way that it wasn't obvious that it held no occupant. Eyeing the electronic keypad, she inquired about the device, "Who has access?"

"The code is the same as the back gate," he shrugged, "So if you ever want to come in from here in the front, you simply type it in. The limo driver has a remote, so he opens it without even stopping, which is probably why you never noticed the missing man. And if anyone else were to come up, without either of those things, the call button goes to Pete, and he can allow access via his little gadget. Overall, it runs just as smoothly as having an actual person here."

Tori swallowed hard, wishing she hadn't asked. "I hope you don't take offense that knowing all of this doesn't make me feel any better. At least tell me that Pete is close at hand."

"Now that, I can do," he chuckled and indicated the garage with a small cottage attached to it. "I'm sure you're aware that the limo driver and gardener reside in there, and Pete also has a room. One of the perks of the job; free housing. Of course, the few other rooms that the other guys held are vacant; not that it really matters."

Tori stared at the small structure, situated a few hundred yards away from the house, nodding slowly, "You stayed there when you worked here?"

"Yeah, as a matter of fact, I did. And you have to understand that all of these things are designed to keep out your typical crazies, star stalkers, and the like," he held his hand up to indicate they should head back to the house. "Things are pretty much the same as when I ran them; it's just all done by one person, with the help of technology."

He wafted his hands at the perimeter walls, "It would be nearly impossible to keep the people you're thinking about out with a typical home system if they wanted in, guards or not. But then again, they don't know where you are, and you took care of the nosey press, so they're a non-issue." He grinned at her, watching her breath frost as she crunched through the snow beside him. "Like I said, we're safe enough. Safe and secure, no doubt in my mind."

"Yeah," she agreed as they reached the door, "I guess you're right." *No sense making a big deal and scaring everyone.* She hadn't had any bad vibes in a while, *maybe it's time I really started believing there are good things in my future, instead of looking for the clouds.*

Gifts Galore

Christmas morning dawned crisp and bright. Cody and Collin were in Nebraska, and Stella was the only other person on the estate, besides Tori, her husband, and her brother, as the limo driver and even Pete had gone for the day. The housekeeper had spent Christmas Eve visiting some family, but had returned to cook a large meal for the three of them to have for their Christmas dinner.

Rising early, the couple hit the gym. Having removed his shirt, he pushed himself with his sweaty, hair covered chest exposed, making it very difficult for her to focus, and causing her to lose count twice during the process. By the end, she lamented that she should be allowed to do the same, see how he liked it.

Laughing at her typical sex driven escapades, Michael took her upstairs, where he finished her with his agile tongue before they moved to the shower for a round against the wall. He deeply enjoyed those encounters, planting her firmly, and then taking his time to satisfy himself after a prolonged amount of slow fucking.

Dressing warmly, the couple set out to explore the small drifts of snow, until Brian awoke and they would be ready to open the gifts that surrounded the base of the massive tree.

Laughing merrily, Tori pelted her mate with snowballs, and then ran from him as he chased her, knowing he intended to throw her down into white powder in retribution. An incredible morning, she tried not to allow her fears that Michael would send her on the road alone to interfere.

Standing inside the kitchen a short time later, the couple enjoyed hot coffee and the smell of their meal as Stella moved around in the bright warmed air to prepare the dishes. Leaning his rear end against the counter, Michael caught the older woman staring at him, and he gave her a small nod and half grin, which caused her to break into a wide smile, and her face flushed. His heart skipping a beat, he wondered what that had been all about, as he turned his attention back to his wife.

"So, what's the plan for New Year's Eve, do you think?" he asked, trying to break the brief connection he had shared with the housekeeper.

Tori sat at the table, going over some sheets of paper, busily working on the lyrics that had been inspired by their outdoor fun. "I don't really know," she replied without looking up.

Relieved his bride had not noted the exchange, he took a seat beside her and fawned over her in an exaggerated manner.

The couple still sat in the wooden chairs, cuddling and cooing in German when Brian entered the room. Retrieving a cup of coffee for himself, he took an empty chair and asked eagerly, "Are we ready for presents yet?" He had gone to great lengths to spoil his sister and her husband and eagerly wanted them to see his purchases.

Taking their mugs, the three of them made their way through the maze, until they reached the front room with a giant tree. Taking the time to divide the packages according to the recipient, they began to open the offerings. A bit daunted at the size of her pile, Tori noted that it easily doubled either of the men's stacks.

Brian laughed at seeing her distress, "Ok, I may have gotten a little carried away."

Using an open palm, she teased, "A little? This looks to be a bit more than a little…"

"Hey, some of those are from me," Michael pointed out.

She smiled brightly at the idea that she could be so loved. Other than the guitar last year, she had never really received presents and struggled with how to go about doing so graciously. "Well, thank you. Both of you." She wanted to convey how important the men were to her, and that their gifts were appreciated, and in her mind's eye, this presented an opportunity for her to learn some manners.

Diving into the mountain of shiny foil, paper and bows, she did her best to open each with equal enthusiasm. However, by the end she found the task difficult to maintain after such an exaggerated number.

Taking inventory, she discovered that she had received new earrings, in bright shiny silver and diamonds, including new studs for the upper parts of her ears that she never traded out, and a few pairs of large hoops that she had never worn before.

She also had been given a variety of clothing she would never have chosen for herself, including felt materials and a few cashmere sweaters. Eyeing the couple of dinky leather skirts, complete with fishnet stockings, she surmised some of the items would never again see the light of day.

Looking over the clothing, she felt relieved that they had stayed with her typical monochromatic tendencies with black, white and grey scale choices. Michael had also given her a large number of lacy undergarments, which caused her brother to shake his head and laugh. Tori laughed with him, glad that Collin and Cody had not been present for the unwrapping of the provocative portion of the spread.

The three of them were still talking and carrying on, when a familiar voice spoke up from the doorway, "Wow, baby girl, tha's some haul."

Swinging around in utter surprise, Tori found herself staring at Brett Spears and Enrique Dominguez, who unsuccessfully tried to suppress his grin at seeing her. "Oh… my… God!" she squealed a little too loudly at his full beard.

Leaping forward, she threw her arms around the taller man, obvious joy at seeing him as she pressed her body flat against his. Her fingers reached to examine his new, shoulder length curls, "What the hell are you doing here? And how did you get in?" The estate was secured, or at least it should have been.

Brett grinned at her, "Same way we got in las' time, minus th' bodies o' course."

Shifting his stance, Brian demanded loudly, "Who the fuck're you guys? And what the hell is going on here?" Michael had told him all of the men who broke into his house were dead, and he quickly surmised that maybe his brother-in-law should have asked after all.

Her gaze shifting from her former lover, Tori could see the tension in her husband's clenched jaw. She had forgotten that the two men had met before, and it occurred to her that he would not be happy to see that she had let the man live, or that she had been so quick to fling herself into his arms.

Nodding at the scene, Michael played it cool, not giving in to his desire to intervene and stake his claim on his wife physically. He had come a long way at controlling his random, jealous thoughts and emotions, and wasn't about to lose it that easily. "Hello," he stated calmly, "So, what brings you here?"

Enrique's sneer a mild challenge, he held the girl about the waist and tossed his head slightly, "We was just passing through." A flat lie, obvious to everyone in the room.

"Is something wrong?" Tori instantly on edge, she knew they would never show up unannounced without a reason.

"You could say that," Brett reached inside his jacket and produced a magazine, opening it so that she could see the cover clearly. "Always took ya for a smart li'l bitch, but this," he smacked the page with his left hand as he held it out with the right, "This was about th' stupidest thing you could do."

Jaw dropped, Tori felt as if she'd been slapped. Sliding out of Enrique's grasp, "I see. Well, that's pretty blunt, and I'm sorry I don't meet with your approval -"

"My approval!?!" Brett's voice grew loud with anger, "Fuck me, baby girl, my approval ain't got nothin' to do with this. If you had laid low, you mighta stood a chance."

Eyes flicking between his accusing glare and the picture, Tori could feel her blood beginning to boil, "You can hold it right there. None of The Organization actually knows anything about me. The only people who do are you two, so unless one of you plans on running off and spilling your guts, I feel relatively safe in this." She defended her actions, even if she wasn't as confident as she hoped that she sounded.

Green orbs fixed on her delicate features, Brett's rage ebbed; "It don' matter, baby girl. You was with th' Dragons long enough, and the few times you was seen with us. Two groups came up dead. I don' know it for sure, but it'd be my guess, The Organization's gonna wanna know why."

Tori flicked her eyes at the floor between them, shifting her stance as she considered his words carefully. *Surely that wouldn't be enough to lead to me.* Chewing the inside of her cheek, she countered "So, you showed up here just to yell at me? Tell me to my face what a bad move this was?"

"Nope!" the word popped out of his mouth crisply, "We're your new bodyguards," he tossed a thumb back and forth between them.

Her eyes shot up to stare at his, "No fucking way. You can't be my bodyguards!" Her voice almost shrill, filled with panic induced by the thought of having either of them close to her on a full-time basis.

"No. No, no, you two don't belong here," her mate quickly interceded, physically moving to intervene, "We have all the protection she needs."

Enrique shook his dark hair vigorously, pointing an angry finger, "You don't gots a choice, man. See, she was mine long before you put your name on her chest, and I'm not about to let anything happens to her." He stared coldly at the other man as he spoke, the challenge clear.

"Thanks, Enrique, for that… endearing evaluation of the situation. But really, we have things covered." She reached up, laying her fingers lightly against his chest, positioning herself between them. "I think either or both of you would have a greater chance of being recognized than I would, and quite frankly," she paused, needing to be diplomatic if she wanted to convince them, "We really don't need your help. We appreciate the thought and thank you for your concern, but it would be better if you left."

The two men looked at one another, Enrique shoving his hands into his pockets angrily.

Face drawn, Brett pursed his lips; "We ain't leavin', baby girl. You want us out; you're gonna have t' turn us in. You said the Feds wanted t' know about us, an' I'm curious how you managed t' take out our entire group without bein' taken in. I figure you cut some kinda deal." His expression calm, the accusation in his eyes tore at her heart. "D'you kill th' Dragons, too?"

Tori loudly sucked the air in through her teeth. Her gaze dropping, she glanced at the checkered tile at his feet, then back at the sneakers of her brother, who stood behind her. *I already told him about my past*, but she still hated to say the words in front of him.

Slowly nodding, she switched to Spanish to cut her sibling out, "Yeah, I took care of them. Tried to bail out myself, but the Feds found me and kept me alive. Saved me, I guess some would call it."

She shifted her glare back to him, allowing her hand to fall from her former lover, back to her side, dropping back to English as well, "I don't want to turn you in. I'm sure they would be glad to have you, but I can't say that I trust them to any real extent."

Brett cracked a wide grin, "Then it's settled. Where do we bunk?"

Brian coughed up a loud, disgusted grunt, "You gotta be kidding me. You two knuckleheads realize you're not getting paid. We have a security team."

Brett stared at him, rolling his tongue as he allowed the younger man to consider his so-called security team, and the fact that he had made it into his house twice. The grin on his face turned to a chuckle, as he watched the estate's owner reach the same conclusion.

Brian glanced over at his sister, who bobbed her head very slowly, looking for her assessment.

"They don't need to be paid. I'm sure they aren't here for the money." Drawing in another noisy breath, she tossed her dark waves, "There's some bedrooms on the second floor. Have your pick, and consider yourselves my guests. Mostly… stay out of the way." She cracked a small smile as the two men grinned at each other, heading out of the room while slapping each other on the back to celebrate their victory.

Michael rocked his jaw side to side as he watched them climb the stairs in the foyer, "What the fuck, love?" he demanded when they had disappeared, "You're gonna move your old boyfriend in, right in here with us? If you want them to stay, at least put them in the servant's quarters. There's room out there for them."

Switching to German, she cooed, "It's ok; they can watch my back, and you can be my husband. Remember? You don't have to worry about protecting me so much, and can focus on being my lover." She smiled, the appearance of the two negating his fear of filling both roles adequately.

Michael only grimaced, staring at the case of steps.

"And I don't want them treated like servants, love," she spoke to both men, even as she addressed her mate directly. "They're my friends. I want you both to remember that." Neither of the men looked pleased to hear the last part, but said nothing more.

Swinging her gaze around the room at the piles of gifts, the day had taken an ominous tone. Reluctantly, she began to gather the things that had been presented to her to carry them upstairs. Following suit, the men picked up armfuls of the haul, leaving the rest of the cleanup to the maid.

See and Be Seen

It only took Enrique and Brett a few minutes to discover which room belonged to Tori and her husband, and then to choose the two rooms on opposite sides of the hall from each other at the far end of the house. Brett laughed at Enrique's suggestion that they do so, quick to point out that she was, in fact, a married woman.

"So?" Enrique countered easily, "She's married before, too, and that didn't stop her from fuckin' the lot of us. She likes spreading it around, and that ring on her hand ain't gonna matters."

Brett stared at him for a moment while giving it some thought, "Yeah, but that was different," he finally conceded. "She wanted something from us back then, and I don' figure we got anything she needs. Therefore, you're only foolin' yourself if ya think she will. Asides, that Michael looked pretty calm considerin' we jus' broke int' th' place an' started makin' demands."

"And?" Enrique challenged, dropping his bag on the bed and beginning to poke around in the drawers and cabinets.

"And, it's guys like that ya gotta watch out for. It ain't th' ones that go aroun' wavin' their arms an' making a ruckus, them's easy to see comin'. It's th' quiet ones that'll

74

stick a knife in your back when ya ain' lookin'." He stopped there, realizing he had described the girl in question, right down to the shiny metal she carried in her boot. "Son of a bitch. I still can't believe I didn' see it comin'."

"Eh, quit beating yourself up over it. She's smooth as they come. Lies like silk, and that tongue of hers is talented in more ways than one, if you gets what I mean," Enrique tried to cheer the older man with his twisted sense of humor.

"Yeah, I guess you're right," he grimaced at the memory of her mouth and the ways that it had pleased him. "She always did make me feel special," he admitted before he could stop himself.

"Yup, it's what made her so unique. I think I'm settled, let's go check out your room," the dark haired man led the way across the hall.

Leaning against the wall, Enrique continued the conversation while Brett put his few belongings away and had a look around. "You really thinks The Organization'll come after her?"

"There's no doubt 'n my mind," his counterpart replied. "Although I did come down on 'er pretty hard. It was more or less inevitable that they would find 'er. Too many loose ends t' ever have been completely hidden. Won' take long though, with her out in the open like this. Damn, this place is nice. Kinda funny that I'm gonna be livin' here, after me and the guys trashed it, an' all."

Enrique tossed his head back, enjoying the chuckle, "You thinks they got anything to eat around here? I could swear I smells food."

"O' course you smell food, ya dumbass. It's fuckin' Christmas, an' this is the richest motherfucker either one o' us has ever met. We're 'bout t' enjoy a meal t' beat all others, mark my words," he pointed a finger at him, "In fact, I think it's time we headed down t' find out what time it's gonna happen."

Tori, busily arranging her new arrivals into her closet, heard the two men when they passed by her door. As their chatter began to fade, she called out down the hall after them, "Hey, you two got a minute?" Seeing them turn, she smiled, "I was thinking I might need to have a quick word with you. Maybe set some rules, since you're going to be staying here and everything."

"Ok," Brett shrugged non-committedly, "Whatcha got 'n mind?"

"Well, I was thinking that if this is going to work, you two need to stay pretty close to me. Like we're friends," she gave a small shrug.

"Well, we are friends, ain't we baby girl?" Brett couldn't hide his disappointment at her choice of words.

"Yeah, we are, but that's not what I'm talking about," she folded a stack of shirts calmly, placing them in a drawer. "I mean when we're out in public; it shouldn't look like you two are guarding me. You know? It should appear more natural, like we're hanging out together, or that you're part of our group."

She paused, her eyes darting between the two men, taking in their rough and tumble appearance with a wrinkled brow. "I don't know; I don't want you looking like yourselves," she finished with a loud puff of air.

Enrique's brow furrowed deeply, "What the fuck's that supposta mean? Who're we gonna looks like if we don' looks like ourselves?"

"You can't look like street thugs," she stated flatly. "You have to blend in. Otherwise, you're no good to me, because you'll draw that much more attention."

Inhaling deeply, Brett could see her point. "Ok, I'll buy that; what's your plan for disguisin' us?" he tried to humor her, fairly certain there was no plan. To his surprise, she did, in fact, have things lined out.

"Tomorrow, I'm going to take you shopping. Get you some clothes," she quickly raked her eyes over the taller man, head to toe.

"Clothes?" Enrique raised his chin, "We gots clothes, thank you very much. And there's nothing wrong with them, either."

"I know," Tori smiled, and stood up straight from her folding, trying to smooth his anger as she sidled up next to him, "But they need to be a little newer. A little fresher, if you get my meaning. You look like you've been out on the road a while." She reached up, absently flicking a ringlet of hair off his shoulder.

"That's cause we have been out on the road a while," he countered, his heart rate jumping at her touch.

"Yeah, I know you have, baby," she cooed as she nodded, stepping closer to him, and his hand automatically landed on her hip. "But if you're going to be here with us, and be good at protecting me, people can't be able to tell that from seeing you." She gave him another smile, and he returned the grin, having caught the word *baby* as it fell from her lips.

With a small shrug, he relented, "Ok, tomorrow we gos shopping."

Her smile widened at his agreement, "Good. Then it's settled. You two can go on, find out if lunch is ready. I'll be down in a few minutes." Putting away the rest of her gifts, she hummed quietly to herself, unable to mask the unmistakable joy their arrival had brought her, even if her husband didn't like them being around.

Half an hour later, the group sat around the dining room table, enjoying the fine meal and discussing their agenda. "So, we have another shopping spree tomorrow, I take it?" Brian tossed out cheerily between bites.

Tori looked up from her plate in surprise, "Well, yes, I had planned on taking these two out to get them some more appropriate clothing. Did you want to come along?" She eyed her brother with mild concern, "You know, I didn't think guys liked to shop, but you always seem to be in the mood for it."

"Naw, shopping is just a means to an end, sis. The key is to see and be seen, out in public. We didn't make much of a stir last time, but getting noticed helps us; publicity is publicity, good or bad," he showed his full set of glowing white teeth as he spoke. "Don't worry, you'll catch on, and as hot as you are, you're bound to get noticed."

"Uh, thanks, Danny," she squirmed in her chair, uncomfortable at hearing her brother describe her in that manner, "What're you two grinning at?" she tossed at Enrique, as he seemed to be enjoying the conversation.

"Oh, I just wants to agree," her former lover admitted, cutting his eyes over at Michael.

Tori observed her husband, eating calmly and watching the group, seemingly oblivious as to what went on around him. *Wow, he seems to be taking their arrival pretty well. Much better than I would have anticipated.* "Ok, then we make a day of it," she agreed to the plan. *Won't it be fun.*

I Spy

Filled with nervous energy, Tori set out early the following morning, taking in a brief run down the block and back before returning to the gym. The crisp air felt good on her face, and she relished in the brief serenity of being alone, aware of being severely outnumbered with the addition of the two men to their group, and it would only get worse when Cody and Collin returned.

Michael, already using the equipment, smiled when she entered, allowing her to fall in easily beside him while they pushed their bodies to the limit. To her surprise, Enrique and Brett also came in before they were finished, and Michael greeted them warmly. Gaping at him suspiciously, she couldn't help but wonder what he was up to.

The entire group assembled in the kitchen at 10:00 am for brunch, and Stella demonstrated why the band loved her. She produced the best omelets Tori had ever tasted, stuffed with cheese and generous bites of ham. Michael again seemed at ease, and it made Tori nervous to see her spouse and the two Scorpions exchanging conversation and banter, as if they were old friends.

Watching the trio, she poured over what she knew about them while she sipped her coffee. Brett was Henry's age, which put him close to fifty, give or take. However, Enrique and Michael couldn't have been more than a year difference in age, and perhaps that gave them more common ground. They were all three former SF as well.

She knew that Enrique had met with her husband previously, before they were married, but considering his story at the moment made her curious. Did her mate know Brett as well? Could there be more to their relationship than he had led her to believe? She didn't like the feeling that her husband had secrets from her, especially if her former lovers were a part of them.

Ready to begin the day's adventure, the five friends piled into the limo, the girl choosing to take the window seat, facing forward. Michael slid smoothly in beside her and placed his hand on her leg. Feeling her husband caress her thigh, she avoided looking at the two men seated across from her, facing the bar. She couldn't help the feeling of being back in the midst of the crew, the tension palpable; almost as if they were each waiting for their turn, and she wasn't sure how she felt about that.

As soon as the actual shopping began, Tori began to relax and took over the two men, making suggestions and pulling out items for them to inspect or try on. Brett blew her off right away. She giggled at the stern expression he wore when he informed her that he knew what he needed and could dress himself.

Enrique, on the other hand, appeared eager to be close to her, and seemed quite willing to have her holding up shirts and pressing them against his broad chest. He liked the way her hands felt through the cloth, occasionally catching her fingers to toy with them, the two of them becoming comfortable to the point of being oblivious to the others in their search for his new attire.

Michael watched the pair warily, pretending to be shopping himself as his cover and maintaining outward acceptance. *The two of them are awfully cozy,* he noted, knowing better than to make a scene. *Can't push her about it, though. Throwing a fit won't win me any points.*

Taking in more than a dozen stores, the car had been stuffed with purchases for the two men, as well as a few items for the rest of them, and Tori found herself laughing out loud as they rode home, "So, when do we have enough?" she teased.

"Enough what?" her brother countered.

"Enough crap," she stated evenly, "Every time we go out, we blow money on more stuff we don't need."

"We need it," he returned her grin. "Think of it this way, we're helping the economy."

"What the fuck kind of excuse is that?" she continued to smile.

"A real one. Seriously, by spending money, we give people jobs. I'm not kidding, and I know it sounds wrong, but when you reach the point, you have more than you could spend in a normal lifetime... it's time for you to spend more." He stared at her, and she thought about his words carefully, still not sure the logic was sound.

"So what do we do when we can't stuff anymore into the closet?" she gnawed at her lip while she considered the issue.

"We donate stuff, to homeless shelters or Goodwill stores," he smiled again, "I'm telling you, we're much more into community service than you probably realize."

The girl nodded slowly, surprised at the simple, yet obvious solution. Giving her husband a quick glance, she saw that he watched her, his expression once again appearing compliant. Choosing German, she inquired quietly, "You ok?"

"Yeah," he gave her a grin while returning his hand to her knee, "Getting there, anyways."

As the car pulled up in front of the massive structure,

Tori had a swarm of butterflies break loose inside her belly as she considered the changing dynamics within the group. Watching the men carry in the bags, she admonished herself firmly, *calm down baby girl, this is a good thing.* But her thoughts did little to bring her scattered emotions under control.

"That's it; they're back inside," Eli spoke calmly. "Guess we should make the call."

Nodding his agreement, Mason Hunt checked his messages. "Yeah, the other team is in position and ready to relieve us. Let's get some coffee and take care of checking in."

The two were seated in a plain, late model sedan, with Eli at the wheel. He had parked along the curb outside the front gate momentarily, and swung his gaze around one last time before pulling back out into the street, "Go ahead; you can put him on speaker. Get this over with," he repositioned his hands anxiously.

Reaching for his phone, Mason pulled up the number and made the call. Touching the button to make it a community conversation, he waited patiently for James Godfry to pick up the line. "Hello, Jim. This is Hunt."

"Yes, Hunt; you have something to report?" Godfry queried, all business.

"Yes, sir; we have an issue. It appears that Dominguez and Spears have rejoined our girl." He paused for a moment, licking his lip as he chose his words carefully, "She took them shopping today, and from the looks of it, they are here to stay."

The two men waited, hearing their commander inhale noisily as he considered the news. "Anything else?"

"No, sir. Only that they arrived and appear to be making

themselves at home. Any advice?"

"None. Keep to the plan, and do not interfere. However, do keep me posted if anything else changes."

"Roger that; thank you, sir." Mason ended the call abruptly, returning the device to his inner pocket and squirming slightly in his seat.

"I have to say, I don't like this," Eli informed his partner. "Their arrival means something."

"Yeah, I think so, too," his counterpart reluctantly agreed, "But what, remains to be seen." He cut his eyes over at the other man, "We informed Godfry, and he didn't alter our orders. That means we continue our surveillance."

"I don't like spying on her. It isn't right." Eli pushed the issue, causing Mason to chuckle.

"You know, I've never met this girl, but I really am curious what she's got that makes men go stupid," he chided.

Keeping his eyes on the road, Agent Founder didn't bother to respond. *I don't see caring about a woman as stupid;* he consoled himself as he pulled up in front of their usual café.

Man to Man

As soon as the new purchases were safely tucked away in her closet, Tori set out to find Brian, eager to share the melody the day had inspired with him. Convincing him they needed to make some music, the pair made their way into the studio for a few hours of jamming out and putting their heads together.

Seeing that his wife and brother-in-law would be out of the way for the duration of the day, Michael quickly decided the time had come for a man to man chat with the new arrivals. Making his way down the hall, he whistled to himself, arriving at the two rooms to find Enrique simply standing, staring at the assortment of packages, and not actually moving to put any of the items away.

"Pretty daunting, huh," Michael commented as he eased his way through the door.

"Yeah, it is," Enrique cut him a distrusted glare, Brett's warning fresh in his mind as the snake slithered into the room.

"Don't worry, you'll get used to it," Michael kept up the friendly façade.

Enrique only nodded, reaching for a sack and allowing the contents to tumble out onto the king sized bed.

"How about some coffee instead? All this shit'll still be

here later. Or you could have Stella put it away."

"Stella? The maid?" the other man scoffed. Pursing his lips, he lifted one of the garments, "Ya know, I gotta be honest with you. I never had anything. Growing up, we was dirt poor. This," he cast his eyes around the room, "This's some shit, man."

"Yeah, I guess so," Michael smiled again, "So, how about that coffee? Let's get Brett and go have a break."

Nodding, Enrique made his way across the hall to find Brett had a large portion of his new wardrobe already stowed. "Woah, you don't mess around."

"Hell no, get this shit done, get settled," he beamed, "We had fun today. Did ya see the look on 'er face?"

Enrique placed his arm above his head on the wall next to him to lean on, "Yeah, I seen it. She was happy today." He glanced over at her husband, checking his expression, "I don't know that I've ever seen her smile like that."

Michael calmly leaned his rear end against the wall facing him, considering the man before him, "I guess you really do care about her after all."

Instantly the other two men were on edge, Enrique pulling his arm down and standing up straight, "What the hell's that supposed t' mean?"

Throwing his arms up to fold them across his chest, Michael only grinned, "It means exactly what it says. You care about her. You want to take care of her. Of course, you realize that she's my wife, or at least I hope that you do." After seeing their familiarity during the day, he needed to evaluate its importance to the future.

Eyes shifting head to toes and back again, Enrique sized him up, "Yeah, I gets it. So you wantin' to go have coffee is just a ruse. Why don't you jus' say what you gotta say already an' be done with it."

Brett grinned, "Oh, are we gonna go have coffee, get all

chummy?"

Michael laughed, surprised by their easy going attitudes, "You know, you guys don't strike me as the badass-wanna-be's the Dragons always came across as."

"That's cause we're not," Brett offered readily, "Eddie Farrell was a mean son of a bitch, an' his brother Red was right there with him. Or maybe it was th' other way 'round, who knows. The point is, we ain't them."

"Right," Michael nodded, "Alright then, let's go grab us some mugs. Discuss the particulars while Tori is busy in the studio with her brother."

"You mean talks about her behind her back," Enrique supplied.

Michael shrugged as he stood up straight, "I guess you could call it that. Let's just say, she don't need to know everything that goes on between us. Let's call it... a gentleman's agreement."

"An' what exactly is it we're agreein' to?" Brett eyed him warily.

"Oh, you know. Stuff that needs to be said," Michael wafted a hand at the pair. "I'll let you guys help decide that. I mean, if we're going to be friends after all, we're going to need to learn to trust each other, right?" Turning his back on them, he strutted down the hall, assuming they would follow.

"You believes that guy?" Enrique kept his voice low.

"Yeah," Brett dropped the jeans he had been tending to on the bed. "He's some piece o' work," and made his way out the door, headed for the stairs.

Finding Michael in the kitchen, working on the pot, Brett nonchalantly took a seat at the table to wait, Enrique following his lead. The trio didn't bother talking while the java brewed, and used the time to evaluate.

When the cups were finally filled, Brett lifted his calmly and inquired if they actually had an agenda for the meeting, causing Michael to release a small laugh.

"I really like your sense of humor, Brett," he stated slickly, "That's good. I have a feeling you're going to need it."

Not bothering to take offense, the older man quickly agreed, "Yeah, it does come in handy. I guess you understand we didn' come here t' hangout in fancy clothes an' sit around drinkin' coffee."

Michael took a sip of his steaming liquid before he replied, "No, I didn't figure you did. And I guess the first thing I want to put out there is; it wasn't really Tori's fault, her being here, playing in the band. Don't get me wrong, she wants it, and she loves the music, but I don't think she would have chosen this if we hadn't persuaded her a bit."

Brett's green eyes lit up, "Persuaded her? You mean you talked her int' doin' this shit? What kind o' idiot are you?"

The other man didn't flinch, "I didn't see it as an issue. She is who she is. Either they will find her or they won't. Living like she's afraid, either way, isn't any kind of life."

Brett leaned back in his chair, watching his lips as he spoke. "Hmm, that's one way o' lookin' at it. I guess that has somethin' t' do with the smile she wears a lot more, too."

Brett voiced his opinion as Enrique nodded his understanding. "So we alls agree that she's in danger then," Enrique clarified the point.

"Yes," Michael stated flatly, "But she doesn't need to live like she's scared. That's what we're here for. We got her back." He lifted the cup in a small toast to the others having stated what he hoped would be the foundation of their friendship. Nodding, the other two men were quick to approve his opinion.

"So that's it then," Brett seemed eager to end the conversation.

"Well, not quite," Michael stood for a refill before

getting to the heart of the matter, "I had one other favor I needed to ask of you guys. Something more important I guess. See, protecting Tori from the bad guys is all well and good, but there's someone closer to her that she needs a little help with."

Enrique tossed his chin up, "Oh yeah, who?"

"Herself."

Enrique's jaw dropped wide open, "Herself? What the hells you mean by that?"

His fingers running around the lip of the warm glass, Michael took his time. "I know you guys are close to her." He cut his eyes over at the younger of the two, "I know you may even have feelings for her. What I would like to do, is to ask you not to act on those feelings."

"Are you asking me to *not* fuck your wife?" Enrique busted out laughing.

Michael's features remained placid, even as Brett also began to snicker. "Yeah," he replied after a tangible pause, "Look, you know how she was raised. She never had a normal life before she and I were married." Pausing, he wiped his mouth with the back of his hand, and then changed tactics. "Ok, let me ask you this... Why did you leave her with me?"

Enrique only stared at him, his laughter subsiding and his brown eyes sparkling while he considered the question.

Seeing that he wasn't going to get an answer, Michael tossed out his theories, "Is it because you felt sorry for her? Because you really *don't* care? Or because you really want what's best for her?"

"Man, you're a real son of a bitch! Ya know that?" Enrique exploded with a burst of anger, giving the table a violent shove to push his chair back to stand, taking the other men by surprise.

Moving over to the sink, he tossed the cup in, causing it

to shatter, which he ignored. Leaning against the counter, he ran his fingers through his hair, drawing a noisy breath in through his nostrils and exhaling it through a relaxed jaw to calm himself. "I ain't gonna promise not to fuck her. Not if she's willin'."

Spinning around to lean his backside on the edge of the sink, he threw his arms across his chest and folded them. "Likes I said, she was mine before she was yours, and maybe I don't likes your definition o' normal. Maybe she don't. If I had it to do over again… I can't says that I'd do it the same. Not after the way things turned out."

Rocking his jaw side to side, Michael tried not to let on how pleased getting the confession had made him. "I'll keep that in mind," being all that he said in reply. Standing, he placed his mug on the counter, using it to move right up next to the other man so he could look him in the eye before he turned his back and exited the room.

Dark Places

Special Agent Mason Hunt stood in the shadow of the tree; his black trench coat wrapped tightly to keep him warm. Peeking out, down the path that she regularly took when she ran, he hoped that today would be such an occasion, and he would get the chance to speak to her alone. Digging in his pocket, he pulled out a cigarette, lighting it and leaning back into the corner formed between the tree and the wall of the estate he had had under surveillance for weeks.

Hope that jackass Founder stays put, he muttered to himself and popped the lighter closed, drawing a deep drag that produced a bright red cherry at the end of his smoke. Adjusting his toboggan to cover his ears more fully, he thought about his latest partner and their current case. The case he had invited himself in on at the request of Terral Huffman.

"Old Terry was right, you know," he talked to himself aloud in a low gravelly voice, "This shit just don't add up." Relaxing into the darkness, he peeked through a small crack between bark and brick, watching the lighted path that she would take, leading to his hiding place. *Somewhere in this tangled mess, there's a connection. This girl's in the middle, so do we trust her?* He took another long drag. *Have to trust her,* he reminded himself again; *we don't have a choice.*

Catching a glimpse of the spandex legs jogging down the snowy walk, Hunt crushed his cigarette against the wall behind him, protecting the glow from being exposed behind the tree. Stepping out when she reached the towering Pine, he spoke sharply, "Tori!" grasping her waist and spinning her into the alcove, back against the wall, perfectly pinned.

The girl stifled the urge to scream, seeing the long coat as he gripped her, her mind racing. "You a Fed?" she stammered, unarmed and aware of her distinct disadvantage.

"Yeah," he breathed, air frosting with excitement. "I'm Mason. Mason Hunt. We don't have time to talk here, but we need to." She pushed herself away from the wall, standing toe to toe with him as he spoke.

"Oh, we need to," Tori's eyes dropped to take in the tall frame, her gaze only staring at his chin at straight ahead, "And what if I refuse?" She noticed the pained grimace that crossed his features in the dim light.

"You can't refuse, baby girl… your life may depend on this."

Her jaw dropped at his words, the tenderness unmistakable. Pushing him away from her, she straightened herself, prepared for battle, "Ok, who the *fuck* are you – really!?!"

Reaching into his pocket, "We don't have time for this." He handed her a slip of paper, "This is a biker hangout. Come dressed the part, and I'll explain everything to you. Midnight." Releasing her, he turned and walked straight across the street and down the path that wound behind the next residence, leaving her staring after him.

Wadding the page and gripping it tightly, Tori jogged easily to the gate and let herself in, cutting her run short with the clang of the metal entrance behind her. Inside the kitchen, she lay the ball on the counter to set up the coffee pot, her fingers trembling as they stiffly complied. *Damn. And here I*

91

thought having Brett and Enrique show up two days ago was bad enough. Fresh Feds wanting to meet with me only adds to the situation.

Exhaling a deep sigh, she watched as the muddy water began to collect in the pot. *Mason Hunt. I don't know him. Never heard his name, either.* Her mind turned the brief conversation repeatedly. *He called me baby girl. Oh my God, I don't believe this shit.* Setting a mug on the counter, she reached for the note.

Opening the crinkled letter, her eyes perused the perfectly scripted letters:

I realize you don't know me, but I'm going to ask you to trust me. I can't say much here, in case this falls into the wrong hands. Meet me at the Red Devil's Bar at the time that I indicated. I think you know it, so dress to blend in. I'll be in the corner at the smaller bar, right-hand side. See you there.

Tori's mind raced. *Yeah, I know the place;* indeed a biker bar, a dark place that she had been to several times with the Dragons. *Filled with guys who think they're tough, and the kind of girls who have a thing for bad boys.* Her mind briefly recalled the women that Eddie or Red had chosen out of the joint, and the places they had dumped their bodies afterwards.

Giving off a small shudder to clear her thoughts, she reached for the steaming brew. Pouring the cup and replacing the carafe, she wondered if she would actually attempt to meet with the stranger. Moving to the window and staring out into the yard, the first light of dawn beginning to glisten across the snow, she contemplated that she didn't really have a choice.

How am I going to pull it off, though? She didn't really want to involve anyone else in the house if she could help it. *I'll have to sneak out. Or come up with an excuse to be out.* She quickly concluded that would be a bad option, as giving any indication that she wanted to go anywhere would have the others wanting to tag along or at least follow her. *I could sneak out; Michael showed me all the security here, and I know how to get around it.*

So, I need a plan. And an outfit. Continuing to gulp the hot liquid, she made a list of things that would be required. *I think I need a skirt. God, I hate those things. But if I want to fit in... yeah, I need a skirt. And some leggings and a pair of those ginormous earrings.*

Her mind quickly leapt to the gifts from Christmas. Smiling to herself, she realized she already had everything she would need piled in her closet. *And here I thought I would never use any of that shit.*

Placing her empty cup in the sink and grabbing the note, she made her way upstairs to shower and dress for the day. She would have to decide how she would ditch the group of men and make it out of the house before the time came. *Jesus, can't I just for a little bit have a normal life?*

Tori leaned against the bar, holding her face in her hands. Everything in place, she carefully laid down the final portion of her plan. From there, she would run upstairs, taking her bag and leaving via the window, where a cab would be waiting for her down the street. The cab would take her to the motel, where she would change before and after the meet.

A few minutes later, Michael's concerned eyes followed his wife as she exited the lounge. *She was complaining about a headache all damn day.* The girl had insisted she didn't need anything before she said her goodnights, but it wasn't even 10:00 pm yet, so her going to bed this early didn't sit well with her mate. *We've pretty much fallen into the routine of the house, so this is damn sure early. Maybe I should check on her in a bit.*

Unable to sit still, he only half listened to the jokes and banter of the other men while he wandered around the room. Hearing his name, he turned to find Enrique holding up a pool cue. "What?" he inquired absently.

"You're up, man," the other replied.

"Oh, umm," he glanced at the door, lost in the idea of caring for his bride. Heaving a deep sigh, he knew she wouldn't like being pestered, especially since she wasn't feeling well. "Sure." He reached for the rack to set up the next game. *It's ok. She's upstairs, she's alone, and you can give her some room,* he chided himself for his overly protective thoughts. *Relax and enjoy the evening,* he instructed himself, allowing the laughter to draw him in.

The Lion's Den

Mason Hunt shifted on his stool inside the Red Devil's Bar. Lifting his glass, he touched it to his lips, watching himself in the mirror across from him. *I need to work this out... see Tori's caught up in this mess, with the FBI pulling on one side, her life on the other. And out in the background, we have The Organization, which is doing their own thing... but what is their own thing?*

Swirling the golden liquid, his thoughts wandered. *Fifteen more minutes. After that, I'm going to bail. I sure thought she'd show.* Lifting the glass, he took a small sip. *Of course, she doesn't really know what's going on, so why would she trust some crazy Fed who shows up out of the blue and demands an audience?* He knew she was in danger, either way.

The Organization is short two groups that used to handle a large portion of their business as far as keeping things running smoothly, and they're not happy about it. Eventually, they're going to get to her; it's only a matter of time. Glaring at the reflection again, he saw her outline, a set of long dark curls, making her way up behind him. Turning slightly, enough to take in her tall frame, his eyes trailed up the long legs covered in fishnet that hid the scars beneath.

Reaching the fitted leather that barely covered her nether

regions, he licked his lip; gaze continuing up, across the flat belly that displayed a cute little stud in her navel, beneath the half shirt that stretched across her rounded assets. *Lips, eyes, hair, oh my God, she's gorgeous!*

"Close your mouth," Tori instructed, sliding onto the seat next to him.

"What?" he spluttered.

Smiling, she leaned closer to him, running her hand firmly across his shoulder, "Your mouth is hanging open, love. You need to close it." Giving him a closer inspection, her eyes roved up and down over his complete uniform, growing confident no one around them would suspect him of being a Fed. Her fingers reaching the nape of his neck, she gave his dark curls a twirl with her fingers. "You want to tell me why we're here, and not in a coffee shop or something?"

Clamping his jaw shut tightly, he stole a glance about him and changed the conversation to Russian, "This is a safe place."

Tori barked a laugh, taking his cue and using the foreign tongue, "Safe? Take a look around. This place is *anything* but safe." Their eyes meeting, he knew what she meant.

"Ok, it's saf*er*. No one will be looking for us here. Were you followed?"

She held her expression, curious who would be following her and why. "No, I wasn't. But I can't stay long. Eventually, the party will end, and I will be missed. They think I went to bed sick, so eventually someone will go to check on me."

"We better make this quick, then," he agreed, and raised his left hand to place it on her hip, his thumb caressing the bare skin of her waist to continue her illusion that they were a couple. "I guess you're wondering *why* I've asked you to meet me here."

"The thought did cross my mind." She watched as he raised the glass, tilting it, but his Adam's apple didn't move.

96

Interesting. "You're not actually drinking that."

"No," he confessed calmly, "Better to keep my wits about me. No one knows I'm here, and if we avoid trouble, it'll stay that way." He gave her a weak smile, "You're very observant. And I have to admit, you did well. That outfit is… fabulous."

Tori glanced down at her chest, only half hidden by her jacket. "Yeah, most of this was given to me at Christmas. Didn't think I would actually ever wear any of it." Her face still tilted down; she cut her eyes up at him, "So, what's up?"

"You're in danger; that's what's up. And there isn't anyone that can help you." His gaze rested on her pretty pink lips, *man no wonder Eli fucked up.* "I'm here to warn you, and to make you an offer of sorts, off the record. Officially, we've been told to stay out if it."

"We?" she raised an eyebrow, aware that his fingers were massaging the flesh along her waist.

"I have a small group of agents with me. We're watching you. Waiting to see what happens." He took another tiny sip of his drink.

Tori removed her hand from him, facing the bar squarely, his palm sliding around to her back as she moved. Leaning closer, so that her shoulder pressed against him, her voice dropped, "You know, I don't really trust you guys, and never have. What makes you think I'm going to start now?"

"Because you don't really have a choice. Look, I know that you're gathering men. And you may think it's wise, and that it gives you some protection. It doesn't." He blinked at her, "It's time to come in. Jim says he offered you a spot with us. Why didn't you take it?"

"A spot? Is that what that was?" her tone grew a bit high, the shock evident. Pulling her voice down, "No, hun. He didn't offer me anything. He asked me to go after The Organization. To move against them, take them out."

His mind raced, *there it is again. Inconsistency where Jim is concerned.* "Ok, well then, I'm offering. Join us. You're fantastic from what I've seen."

"What's that supposed to mean?" her eyes narrowed, she watched his tongue slide around his lips.

"It means I have a lot of respect for you." Pulling his hand away from her, he ran it through his dark hair. "Ok, enough. We don't have time to play cat and mouse." He flicked his gaze over at her, aware that being too honest could cost him in the end. *Fuck that, I'm going to have to trust someone in this mess at some point, and my gut is telling me it needs to be her*; he wrangled with himself for a moment, then took the plunge.

"I told you who I am. I didn't tell you why I'm on this case." Tori bristled but allowed him to continue. "About a year ago, I got a call – No, wait, I need to go further back. Well, not yet." He wiped his palm on his jeans, "I'm here because Terral Huffman asked me to look into some things. He and my father were good friends, way back when, and I've known him my whole life."

"When he called me last year, he told me that Jim Godfry was up to something. Now, Jim has always been a 'by the book' kind of guy, but the last few years, there have been rumors. Cases that he's overseeing suddenly coming to a close, and not the way we want them to." He shifted to look her in the eye, "And Terry didn't like some of the things that were being done to you."

"He knew? That they were falsifying my records?" Tori bit the words, anger flashing in her shiny blue orbs, while she struggled to keep her voice under control.

"I don't think he knew any details," he shook his head to reassure her, "But what he did know put him on edge. Especially after he got to know you. I think that's why he called me, and I started snooping around." His mind flashed the video surveillance footage from the hospital, "I saw the film of you at Mercy… you in the gym, you in the courtyard. Suffice it to say, I got a feel for who you are."

Her jaw dropped slightly before she could clench it, "Me in the gym?"

"Yeah, that little gym there in the hospital. You went in every morning, spending an hour pushing yourself beyond belief. And turning your back on that mirror that covered the wall, like you couldn't bear to look at yourself. Plus, all those hours you spent out in the garden, just sitting and thinking." He smiled, "I figure you must have had a lot on your mind."

Tori nodded, "Yeah, I did." Shifting to have a glance around, she could feel her patience growing thin. "So they were spying on me."

"Not exactly. Those were security videos from the public areas. Not in your room or anything like that. Anyways, I started snooping around, checking into the facts from what I could get my hands on, which wasn't much. Jim had the case classified, for national security, which meant most everything requires clearance. It also meant that he was notified that I was doing so."

He chewed the inside of his cheek, aware that he didn't want to show her all of his cards. "I was finally able to push my way onto the team, and I guess you can tell, I don't trust any of them either."

Tori cracked a wide smile, "Yeah, you're looking pretty unofficial here and in that getup. Why would you go to such lengths, I'm wondering?"

"Because in the end, I don't really know who we can trust, any more than you do. So how about it? Make it official and join us?"

"Not a chance," Tori reached over, grasping his glass and downing the shot that had been tempting her since she took her place beside him.

"I figured as much," he shook his head slightly. "Then make me a promise. Watch your back. The Organization is going to make a move against you; I'm pretty confident of that."

"What makes you think so? They don't know who I am, or where to find me. How and why would they come?" she defended herself once again, recalling that Brett had said practically the same thing Christmas Day.

"Oh, you are so naïve," his lips drew into a thin line. "They will; you mark my words. I can't say how or when, but I assure you, it will happen. Watch your back, baby girl."

Tori's eyes snapped to his, aware that he had called her by her nickname previously as well. "Sure. Anything else?"

He cracked a slow, wide grin, ready to let her go, their good-bye kiss at hand. Rising, he stood next to her, the few inches in height he held on her negated by the heels of her boots. His eyes swimming, he slid his arm around her, roughly pulling her against him, nuzzling her slightly with his nose before he covered her mouth with his own.

Tori's hand shot up to his chest, holding pressure against him as if to push him away. Her heart pounding out of control, she became aware that his fingers had found the bottom edge of her skirt on the back side, and were sliding along the folded flesh beneath it. Pulling her mouth free, she punched his chest with her palm, and he breathed, "Run, now, make it look good as you go."

Freeing herself, she realized this was all part of the show, and he had given her an out, so that she could leave in a huff, and none would be the wiser as to the nature of their visit. "You son of a bitch!" She cursed him loudly, her fist making contact once more before she spun on her heel and marched towards the exit, pulling her leather cover back into place as she moved through the crowd.

Secret Lives

Reaching the cool night air, Tori fought to hold the rush of adrenaline in check. It had been months since anyone besides Michael had touched her so intimately; *sorry bastard*, she cursed the agent under her breath. She felt angry at him for putting his hands on her, but even more so at herself, aware that his simple caress had instantly sent her body into overdrive, and she could feel the wetness forming between her bare thighs.

Waving down a cab, she fell into the back seat, struggling with the desire he had kindled so easily within her. *You're such a slut;* she berated herself. *You just met the guy, and you're already aching to take him into a back room...* her mind danced around the memory of the little bar in LA where she and Enrique had first had their fling. Swallowing hard as she stared out the window, she knew she was in trouble.

The car pulled up at the little motel, and she quickly exited the cab, shoving an extra fifty into the old man's hand, "Keep the change. Wait for me, and I'll double it." Her heels clicking as she moved, she slammed the door harder than she intended, making it into the bathroom as her clothes fell to the floor.

Inside the shower, she washed the makeup from her face

and the sticky ooze from between her legs. *Oh my God, why do I react that way? Jesus Christ, this shit is getting old!* Cutting off the flow, she stepped out and hurriedly dried herself. Re-covering her body with her normal attire, she shoved the disguise into her pack and exited the room, leaving the door key on the dresser.

Taking her place inside the taxi, surprised he had actually waited, she gave him the address for the house, and flicked a crisp one-hundred dollar bill at him. "Thanks for waiting."

"No problem," he grinned knowingly as he pinched the bill between two fingers, accustomed to the rich women of the area and their late night exploits. "I'll have you home in no time."

Tori leaned back in the seat, her pulse dropping to a more normal level. Her dark thoughts pulled her countenance into a twisted frown, her mind going over her brief conversation with Special Agent Mason Hunt. *I knew Jim couldn't be trusted. I wonder if he'll sick The Organization on me, since I refused to do what he asked.* The thought scared her a little, and pissed her off even more.

I have to figure out how to do this; she bit her lip as she formulated her plan. *I sure as hell don't want to tell anyone how I got my information.* She also didn't feel right about calling things off with the band either. *This is my life; God damn it! Why the fuck can't I live it in peace?* By the time she reached the house and let herself in the back gate, she knew she wasn't going to say anything to anyone.

Climbing up to the window she had exited from only a few hours before, she slid the pane up quietly. Poking her head inside, she could see the bed still flat, and undisturbed. *Good, there's a solid chance I wasn't missed.* Dropping her pack into a corner of the closet, she grabbed the blankets on the bed, dragging them about and creating a disheveled look to the place.

Moving into the bathroom, she stripped down, stepping into the shower for the second time, and pushing her dark curls beneath the stream, none too soon. Hearing the bathroom door close loudly, she turned to see her husband peeking around the curtain.

"You ok?" his brown eyes filled with concern.

"Yeah, I think so. I got sick to my stomach. Threw up everything we ate today," she lied smoothly, adding a bit of tremor to the hand she reached out to him with for effect.

Catching the trembling fingers, he rubbed them firmly before he kissed them. "Do I need to change the sheets?" he asked softly, his face still drawn in lines of worry.

"You might check them," she nodded her agreement, "Think I made it, but just in case." She gave him a weak smile, thankful he had no clue what she had been about for the night.

Leaving her, Michael made his way out to the pile of bedding and began to pull at the blankets, inspecting them carefully. Finding nothing out of place, he put them back on the bed, smoothing them down as his mind considered his wife's sudden illness, suspecting food poisoning as the culprit.

Tori exited the small room a short time later, wearing nothing but a bath sheet. Finding him still awake, lying on his back and staring at the ceiling, she caught her breath at the sight of his hair covered chest. Slithering in from her side, she moved all the way across, spooning her naked body up against his, on fire for the second time that night. Her fingers finding their way into the thick curls that obscured her name, she sighed quietly.

His arm sliding around her, he pushed his face against her damp hair in the dim glow of the small lamp. "Feel better?" he whispered, his soft voice meant to comfort.

"Yeah, actually a lot better," she replied smoothly and

dug her hand down below the edge of the sheet in search of his manhood. Her action surprised him, and he shifted as if he were going to push her away. She lifted her face, grasping with her left hand as he swelled at her touch. Using her right hand to hold him in place, she pressed her lips against his, the coarseness giving away her sense of urgency.

Having gotten him to full attention, she wasted no time moving to straddle him, pinning him beneath her and taking him into her dripping folds. Pushing against him roughly, she proceeded to fuck him as heavily as she could muster, his hands grasping and holding her, a perplexed expression dancing on his features. Allowing her to drive her body against his for several minutes, her loud grunts finally got the better of him, and he grabbed her, forcing her to hold still.

"What the hell is wrong with you?" his eyes narrowed, completely confused by the abrupt shift from sick to horny as hell.

"I… uh… dunno," she pushed her hair out of her eyes, "I'm… you know." Her jaw dropped slightly, "What? I can't be in control once in a while?"

He stared at her, evaluating her words, "Sure, you can be in control. But this is damn sure not like you. Especially considering you were sick all fucking day and puked your guts up less than an hour ago."

Overtaken by a wave of rage, Tori snapped, "So what? I was sick, and I feel better. And, I wanna fuck. I mean, like pound the shit out of me fuck. But I know you're not really *into* that shit, so I gotta do it myself." Her palm pressing against his chest, she pushed herself up to adjust her angle, "You don't mind, do you?" she demanded as she slapped against him once more.

Rocking his jaw, he allowed her to satisfy herself against him, her behavior still out of line with his understanding of the situation. When she had finished with him, she rolled over and turned her back, staring at the window she had slipped through only a short time before. Extending a muscular arm, he cut off the light with a crisp snap, "You're welcome," not at all pleased by the turn of events and wondering if one of the other men in the house had anything to do with it.

Locked Up

The following morning, Tori tried to carry on, business as usual, hitting the gym early and pushing herself to the limit. The atmosphere felt far from relaxed, once again forced to share the space with her husband and two former lovers at the same time. Finishing up her workout, she leaned against the wall to drink water and watch the men as they moved about the room.

She noticed that there seemed to be some kind of silent competition going on between the younger two. Brett appeared to be ignoring them, lost in his routine and content to keep to his norm. Michael and Enrique, on the other hand, were obviously at war.

Watching the pair, she could see them alternating pushups and sit-ups, sets that increased by one each time they switched. It would normally be an activity with a set number of rounds or length of time for completion. After fifteen minutes, she felt confident that neither one wanted to be the first to stop, so the contest continued.

Growing concerned, she made her way over to the men, placing her hand on a rack to lean on. "How much longer are you going to be at this?" she posed the question with a hint of animosity.

Cutting his eyes over at her, Michael focused on keeping

his count to the end of the set before replying, "I guess I could be done. We have plans for the day, love?"

Enrique pulled up as well, "If you gos anywhere, make sures you let us know. We can't looks after you if you don't."

Her eyes darting between them, she grunted at their childish behavior, "I guess we'll see what comes after breakfast." Turning her back, she exited the gym to have her shower in private, essentially leaving them to work out their differences amongst themselves. She was tired of men who fought over her, and unwilling to put up with it again.

Arriving in the kitchen a short time later, she discovered Brian already there, "Wow, you're up early! What gives?"

"I dunno," he grinned broadly, "I woke up this morning with a song in my head. One I can't ignore. You wanna hit the studio with me; see what we can make of it?"

Tori nodded, understanding the desire to deal with an idea when it cried to be heard. Besides, it would make a nice distraction from the silent war that had been taking place between the other members of the household. Hastily having a quick meal, the pair passed Michael as he entered the room, and she gave him a rundown on their plans.

Locking his jaw, he gave her a shrug, "No worries, baby girl. I may come and hang out with you for a bit if you don't mind." His hint of a pout completely adorable, it gave him completely away.

"Sure, anything you like," she replied with a peck on his cheek. He had not been much for watching the band work before the arrival of her friends, but things were in motion within the house, and she could feel the changes moving slowly within the dynamics of their group.

Taking up their instruments inside their sanctuary, the siblings put their hearts into laying out the new melody. She felt quite taken with the lyrics that her brother had pieced together, and they spent the better part of the day putting with them the sound that really brought them to life.

Barely taking a break to eat, they were completely finished with the song as dinner approached, and her brother announced that they needed to set it aside and let it congeal, "Then we can come back to it in a few days and see what we think," he grinned at their accomplishment.

"Yeah," Tori agreed, "I have to admit, I like it a lot."

"Me too," he agreed. "But it's time for me to go. I have a date tonight," he gave her a wink as he shared the news.

Tori chuckled, well aware that for her bandmates, the word *date* would be synonymous with *conquest*, and she would not be seeing him again until sometime the next day if all went well. Leaving him to his recreation, she made her way down the hall to discover the other three members of the household were in the lounge, taking turns shooting pool and keeping tally of the games on a napkin.

"Mind if I join you?" she queried, the last time she and her husband had played tickling the back of her mind.

"Not at all," Enrique spoke for the group, "We ordered sandwiches from Stella if you wanna go tells her what you want. It'll be your turn when you gets back."

Tori hummed softly to herself as she made her way to the kitchen to do precisely that, still somewhat amazed that her husband would be getting along so well with the other two men. She hated to think of her mate as deceitful; but given his jealous tendencies in the past, she could hardly imagine his behavior as anything else. His keeping the battle below the surface was a definite sign that he was up to something, no doubt.

Returning to the party a short time later, she selected her cue and found the chalk, "What're we playing for?" she asked casually.

"Hundred a game," Brett spoke up, leaning his stick

against the bar to slide onto a stool. "We'll settle up at the end o' the night," he grinned at her sheepishly, indicating the board that revealed he was not the most skilled player in the room.

"Your rack," Enrique called to her. "And we're playing nine ball," he added smoothly.

"Nice," she replied, pulling out the spheres and arranging them into a diamond. "You know, we could be partners."

"Naw, we should stick with this," he grinned at her, obviously enjoying the double meaning, whether she had intended it or not.

"Ok," she removed the plastic form and stepped away, "I'm easy."

The last two words caused an awkward silence, as her opponent shot her a funny look before he revealed a slow smile, "You says it, baby girl." Giving a few practice swings, he cracked the rack and ran the table, without giving her a turn at the balls.

Glaring at him, her forehead crinkled, "You guys have spent way too much time playing this game, I think."

Brett snorted a laugh, and Enrique joined in, recalling that the girl had spent far more time laying across pool tables than she had actually playing on them. Her eyes darting between the two men, she returned her cue to the rack and accepted her plate from the housekeeper; "It's all good. I was hungry anyways."

Enjoying the meal, she ate her meat, cheese and crackers wearing a small pout. During Michael's turn, he caught a lucky break. Actually able to have a shot at the balls, he put Enrique out with a devilish grin of satisfaction. "Brett, old man, you ready for another go?"

Brett nodded as he wiped at his face, "Yeah, I'm no quitter, even if I am five-hundred in th' hole," and he laughed to emphasize the point.

Enrique took the chair next to Tori, his leg brushing along hers as he slid into his seat.

She stiffened slightly at the rush of excitement the contact produced. Keenly aware the action had been on purpose, she shifted her gaze to catch him watching her. She swallowed her bite, their eyes locked, and his hand found her leg beneath the wooden surface. "What're you doing?" she demanded quietly, trying to avoid being overheard.

He continued to sneer, giving her a small shrug as the digits pushed over to finger her folds of flesh through their covering, "Nothin'," before he removed the appendage to grasp his dinner with both hands.

Michael watched the two of them, his thoughts churning; he could see the hand return to her leg a short time later. *Dumbass, don't he know I can see him fondling her from this angle?* The other man either didn't know or didn't care, and his hand moved up and down the denim, squeezing and massaging her as they spoke to one another.

The distraction had been enough to throw off his game, and Brett won his first match of the night with a loud, gratified whoop, "Haha, no skunk for me!"

Taking the seat opposite his wife, next to the man who groped her, "You're up, love."

Tori finished her last few bites and moved to rack the balls for the second time. "Well, you look pretty pleased," she teased Brett fondly, her pulse thumping in her neck at the havoc Enrique had put her in with his wandering fingers.

"Yup," he replied. "As long as I win one, I'm good."

Leaning over to situate the spheres, her rear end stuck out slightly, pointing at the two men seated at the table behind her. Michael shifted his gaze to see the other man leering at his bride without the slightest effort to disguise his desire. Puckering his lips, he recalled their conversation only a couple of days prior, when Enrique had boasted he would be more than happy to fuck her, "*if she's willing*" he had said; he felt pretty confident his wife would be willing.

Eating his meal hurriedly, he excused himself before the game had been completed, "Listen, guys; I'm not feeling real well, think I'll turn in." Not waiting for a reply, he left the three of them staring after him, his mind racing, certain she would choose to remain below.

Arriving at their room, he glanced calmly behind him to discover that he had been correct in his deduction. *Yeah, I knew his being here was going to be trouble.* Making his way inside, Michael removed his shirt and pants, stretching out on their king sized bed to stare at the ceiling.

I obviously can't keep her locked up; he ran his hand through the hair on his chest. Images of his wife, naked and alone with the dark haired man tore at him. *You know the odds are good they will have their fling;* he rationalized with himself, *what you have to do is figure out how to win in the end. Or at least... not lose it all.*

Back in the lounge, Enrique finished his meal and sidled up to the dark haired beauty, "Hey, baby girl; why don't you lets me teach you a little bit?"

She stared at him; wide-eyed surprise at what he might be getting at. "Teach me what?" she stammered, her mind still not fully on the game.

"How to play," he indicated the table with an open palm. "Here," he looped an arm around her waist to guide her into position. "Like this."

Brett stepped back from the table, deciding to enjoy his dinner and watch the show. He grew curious if he would get a turn after Enrique had finished with the girl, provided the younger man could get her clothes off now that they were 'alone.'

"Relax, baby girl; I'm not gonna hurts you," Enrique breathed in her ear, his body pressed against her from behind as he guided her.

"I know," she exhaled loudly. "It's been a long time since anyone but Michael touched me, that's all." *Oh my God, what the hell am I doing?* His hand felt warm through the cotton of her shirt, and she could feel her brain go fuzzy at the thought of removing the material.

"We're playing pool," he teased quietly. "Don't grip it so tightly. That's it, lets it slide smooth. That's better."

Taking her through a few shots from different positions and angles, she could easily see that his proximity had the opposite effect, and she actually had gotten worse. "You're distracting me, baby. Why don't you go sit and watch from over there?" she indicated a stool next to the bar with the cue.

"Cause, I likes it better over here," he ran his hand across her ribs as she turned to face him, his fingers tickling her breast and causing the nipple to stand out in a point. "You missed me, didn' you…"

Catching his fingers, she held them still, not bothering to push them away. Cutting her eyes over at the older man, she could see him making quite a show of eating and ignoring their foreplay. She dropped into Spanish, keeping her voice low, "It doesn't matter, even if I did. You know Michael and I are married. Why're you putting your hands on me?"

"Cause you likes it," he grinned broadly, "Besides, your ol' man went to bed and left you here alone with me, so's I don't figure he cares… if you get what I means."

Instantly, she could feel the rage and shoved him away from her, "The fuck if he doesn't care. He trusts me, so back the hell off or get the fuck out!" Clutching her cue, she moved around the table and took another shot while the two men exchanged glances.

"Sorry," he stammered, "That was outta line. I'll try to keep my hands to myself."

"Yeah, see that you do," she continued with the game,

her mind still clouded by the confusion that his touch had produced.

Taking a few shots himself, Enrique sank two balls, then missed the third. Leaning over to make hers, Tori cast a quick glance to find him peering down her shirt, her pink rose glaringly obvious.

The distraction more than enough, the cue ball didn't even make contact with her target, and he laughed, "I'm tellin' you, I could help you."

Straightening slowly, she glanced at Brett to find that he studied her calmly, and it occurred to her that she could fuck the both of them if she wanted to. The idea caused her great concern, and she chastised herself bitterly, considering that a good wife doesn't want to fuck other men. She could see that a good wife only has eyes for her husband, and she thought about her mate's question of her being a cold hearted bitch.

The idea of having either of them placing their hands upon her excited her, and she looked back at Enrique with a slight pout on her lips, "I don't need that kind of help. In fact, I think it's time I went to bed." Laying her cue stick on the table, she avoided moving too closely to either of them as she slipped out the door and bolted for the stairs.

Tori awoke the next morning alone. She had slipped into bed the night before without disturbing her husband, but it had taken a while for her body to cool off from the fire Enrique had so easily kindled within her.

Lying on her side, studying the window, she could see a light snow falling and brushing the panes of glass. Biting her lip, she thought about her choice to leave the man downstairs. Not only last night, but the time she had left him standing on a street corner, when he had begged her to stay. *'You don't need him,'* his words echoed in her mind.

He had been talking about Michael, trying to convince her that he could give her everything she could ever want or need as well, if not better, than her mate. *I could say the same about you;* she argued with him bitterly as she toyed with her wedding band, hating the idea of needing either of the two men. Drawing a deep breath, she closed her eyes for a moment then slid out of the warm bedding to face the day.

Taking a cold shower, she tried to invigorate herself, noticing the dark smudges beneath her eyes before she covered them with her makeup. Putting on her typical jeans and tee, she thought about the places that Enrique's fingers had lingered, only causing her brow to furrow deeper with guilt. Making her way downstairs, she formulated her plan, resolute to demonstrate to everyone where her loyalties lay, including herself.

Arriving in the kitchen, the girl discovered the two Scorpions enjoying their breakfast at the table while her husband stood at the window, coffee mug in hand. Silent as a cat, she crept up behind him, "Good morning, love." Reaching out to him with velvet fingers, she wrapped her arms around him from behind and cooed into his ear.

Michael stiffened at her touch, allowing his digits to run along the backs of her arms as they held him. "Good morning." His words were flat, revealing nothing of the turmoil that raged inside him as he held his gaze, watching the snow drift to the ground.

Pushing her hands across his chest, she hugged him tighter, which drove his anger over the top. Catching her right palm as it massaged her name through his shirt, he broke her hold on him and twisted free.

Turning so he could look at her, he forced a weak smile. "Coffee's ready," and moved out of her grasp to take a seat at the table. "So, still two days until New Years, wonder what that crazy brother of yours will have planned for us next."

Clenching her jaw, Tori moved to retrieve her own cup of java, briefly recalling that she rarely drank the stuff before she came to live in this house and this life that weighed so heavily upon her. "No idea," she answered him absently. "He had a date last night, so there's no telling if he's even home, much less when he'll be joining us."

Nodding, Michael agreed, "All right. Then I think it's time the three of us started discussing actual security. I don't think what Pete has in mind is satisfactory, and I really would like to get your opinions, since you're officially here to help." He wafted a hand at the other two men, and Tori could feel the stab of displeasure wrench her gut, having effectively been dismissed from the conversation.

"Well, sounds like you'll be busy then," she spoke softly, noticing that all three of them avoided looking at her. "Guess I'll find something to keep me busy."

Leaving them to their confab, Tori made her way outside for a lengthy walk about the yard, her mind turning, pouring through old remembrances and forgotten times she had shared with the men of her life. Eventually, she made her way inside, taking her place in the studio. Choosing an instrument, she poured out some of the saddest music she had made in weeks. Her mind still turning, she waited to see what would happen next; both with herself, and with two men she no longer felt like she could choose between.

Happy New Year

Cody and Collin arrived home New Year's Eve morning, ready to celebrate in their customary fashion; a large party and all that it entails. Finding the two newest members of the household only a bit of a shock, they had their own agenda to worry about, and accepted the men without much of a fuss.

That night, the party went smoothly, with lots of guests and hot women for the men to have their pick of. Michael could see the way that Enrique followed the one that belonged to him, openly leering at his bride. He could feel the anger sweltering inside of him, but took great pains to hide his displeasure, as having his feelings on display would not help him in the end.

He had been watching the couple for days, trying to decide how to handle the situation and ensure that he came out on top. He had found a solution of sorts, and had been working on the courage to present his plan to his wife. Fairly certain she wouldn't take the news well, he hoped she at least put up somewhat of a fuss. Part of him feared that she wouldn't, loving the idea, and that thought disturbed him even more.

Tori appeared to be avoiding Enrique, and it caused Michael pain when he considered the possible causes for her behavior. She had made numerous attempts to be overly affectionate with her husband, in public, but behind closed doors, their romance had stalled, which only added to the appearance of guilt.

He hated to think of her as a conniving wench, but in the end, he knew who and what she was. She had become moody, and the couple hadn't been tender in private since her former lover had arrived in the house, leaving her husband little doubt that his presence had been affecting her.

The group held a large toast for the New Year, with cheers, streamers and the like at midnight. Immediately after, Michael suggested that the two of them retire, his resolve firmly in place. Tori agreed, her drawn features doing little to mask her displeasure with her current circumstances. She led the way to their quarters, nervous excitement bringing a tense smile to her lips.

Inside their room, the girl could sense the discourse between them. Tori felt reluctant to get undressed, feeling a bit forlorn, and unsure how to handle the new dynamic that had presented itself within the house. So far, she had avoided Enrique and any further groping on his part, but in only two days of doing so, she had come to realize it wasn't a real solution to the problem; she had become trapped, with no easy way out. More than anything, she wanted to be with her husband, and to know that they were on solid ground.

"So, this is a new year. New beginning," Michael smiled at her, ready for them to have the talk that they had been avoiding.

"Yeah," she nodded as she stared out the window at the white world below, "I guess you could call it that."

Sidling up beside her, he brushed her hair out of the way so he could see her profile more clearly. "You know, we haven't really made love since they got here." He chose to ignore her little escapade the night she had been ill. "Are you afraid that he will hear us? Or are you too lost in thoughts of him?"

Tori cut her eyes over at her mate, finding his questions blunter than she would have liked, curious how she should respond. Blinking at him for several minutes, he appeared ready to wait the entire night if he had to. Opening her mouth to explain, the words tumbled out, "Help me." Her reply surprised her, and her expression shifted to horror, as that had not been what she thought she was going to say. She had never asked anyone for help in her entire life, why would she do it now?

Michael grinned at the utterance, reaching to turn her to face him and pull her against his chest. Palms moving up and down her spine, he squeezed her firmly; reassured more by those two words than by any other she could have said. "I'm here, baby girl." Hands sliding up into her thick tresses, he found her sensitive hairline and caressed the nape of her neck. "I love you so much. You know I would do anything for you."

Tori didn't find the comfort in his attempted reassurance. "Anything?" she managed to reply, "That leaves a lot of territory for things to go awry."

He laughed, "Yeah, it does, but it's ok. I mean it. And as long as we have each other, the world around us can go on about its business. You know what I mean?" His words were his attempt to draw her out, "So tell me, what is it you need?"

"What if it's not that simple?" she countered immediately, her chest heaving nervously. "What if, what I need is more than I have any right to?" she glanced down at his lips, clinging to him. "Michael, I'm not sure how this is going to work out. There are too many variables here now. Things were moving pretty much in a straight line; at least I thought they were. But then Enrique showed up, and I hate to say it, but I feel all torn up inside. And I don't want to go through that again."

"Through what again," he prodded gently.

"Thanksgiving. The night before it, when I dreamed I had lost you. It was so real, and I knew that you were the one thing on this earth that ranks above all others." She paused, aware that her feelings for the other man in the house were tearing at her, not as strong as her love for her mate, but a force to be reckoned with.

"So ask him to leave," Michael stated the obvious solution.

Tori's jaw dropped, air caught in her lungs; "I can't do that!"

"Why not?" he remained calm, having fully expected the response.

"Because," she shifted her stance, trying to free herself from his grasp, "There's lots of reasons. And I don't want to argue about any of them." She stared into his eyes, becoming aware that she did not hold all the cards in the conversation. "I'm not ready to send him away."

"Obviously, there's more to it than that," he didn't want to accuse her of anything, but he had seen the turmoil ripping at her; at both of them.

"Yeah, I guess there is…," she dropped her tone, "He's still in there, somewhere, eating away at me. I won't say that I love him, but he has a hold on me." Her lip quivered slightly, "I broke my vows to you before, and I don't want to do it again… I do love you, even if I'm not very good at showing it."

He stared at her lips, "So, why do you keep your distance? If you're not interested in fucking him, and you are in love with me, why aren't we making love right now? Why are we even talking about this?"

Her jaw dropped, the air hanging in her chest, "I…" she stammered, "I want something you can't give me. Can't or won't. And I don't want to put that pressure on you," she shook her head, still riddled with guilt at her desires, "And I don't want to feel the disappointment when we're done... and you didn't give it to me; no matter what the reason." Her crystal blue orbs grew misty, filled with the pain of her dilemma. "I don't know what else to say, love."

Leaning his forehead against hers, Michael felt stuck. *Time to suck it up. She's yours, and you're going to love her either way.* "You know, these arms belong to you, and they will hold you whenever you need it. I'm sorry I can't be that guy you think you need, and do those things to you your body seems to crave. Just promise me one thing..." he paused, inhaling deeply, preparing for the fallout, "Don't ever make love to that man."

"What?" her voice cracked and he gripped her more firmly to prevent her from pulling away.

"I said, don't ever make love to him," he whispered the words a second time, battered by the idea of her lying with him. "I'm not giving you permission to go fuck him. But I don't want to give you ultimatums. I want you to be free to make your choice without being afraid of what I will say or do. I love you, either way."

Tori tore herself free of him, stepping back, "No, that's exactly what you're doing. What the hell is the matter with you? What kind of man tells his *wife,* 'don't make love to him?' You know damn good and well that implies that it's perfectly ok if I fuck him, like you don't give a shit if I do."

"I do give a shit, ok? Believe me, this isn't something that I have decided on a whim," his lips were drawn down into a deep frown, "But I cherish you deeply. The hardest part for me is whether or not I want to know about it when it happens."

She stared at him, with mouth gaping and eyes wide. "When it happens. You already assume that I have, or that

I'm going to!" The pain the knowledge brought her was unbearable. *He knows you're a filthy whore, and it's only a matter of time before you prove it.* Anger flooded her crowded thoughts. "You son of a bitch. How could you say that to me?"

Feeling the flush of rage welling inside, Michael fought to maintain control, his hand waving about and accentuating his tirade, "You can call me what you like. And you can be and do what you like. I'm trying to *allow* you to be who you are! Fuck him. Don't fuck him. That's up to you. Just leave me out of it. And don't forget where you belong!" He spun on his heel and marched into the bathroom, closing the door with a slam.

Tori could feel the pulse pounding in her ears. *Happy fucking New Year's.* She turned back to the window, pressing her brow against the pane, raising her arm over her head. She wanted to cry, or scream, or break something, in her fit of fury. Staring out into the darkness, she found herself unable to do any of them.

How could he say that shit to me? Does he really think they could just... share me? Or does he think I will get it out of my system and eventually send Enrique away... Listening to the shower, she considered the man standing beneath the steamy torrent in utter disgust. *My God, men and their head games.*

Get with the Program

New Year's Day dawned crisp and bright, and Tori made a point to hit the gym hard, trying to burn off the extra energy she had accumulated through the tension of the household. *Of course, my husband inviting me to fuck my bodyguard hasn't helped matters either*, she fumed as she stormed through twelve sets of twelve pushups, pull ups, and toes to bar leg lifts.

Speak of the devil, she thought wryly as he entered the room while she finished her set. She could guess at his reasons for doing so, but she still wasn't happy about it, and fully intended to prove that she didn't need the other man, despite what her mate thought. Giving him a half sneer, she forced the words, "Good morning," before she left him to his own punishments within the walls of her refuge.

After a quick shower, she made her way to the kitchen, surprised to find Brett at the table drinking coffee, the housekeeper seated next to him. Hanging back at the corner, out of sight, she eavesdropped long enough to realize they were deep in conversation, a small stab of jealousy rearing its ugly head before she squashed it.

"Hey, guys," she called out briskly as she bounced into the room, "Oh no, no need to get up," she waved to the older woman, who was already out of her chair, "I can get my own breakfast, you enjoy your morning." Giving her a smile, the girl hoped her previous thoughts remained hidden as she reached for a plate to serve herself from the dishes that covered the stove.

"I ain't used t' bein' part o' the household so much," she drawled as she reclaimed her seat. "But turns out, me an' Brett here has a lot in common." She smiled brightly, and Tori wondered if the woman's bed could be one of them.

"That's good to hear," Tori held her grin firmly in place, "Actually, I think you and Danny get along pretty well, too," she recalled seeing their friendly banter often, "Well, Brian I mean. Sorry, I forget that everyone else uses his new name."

"That's quite alright child; I understan'. An' yes, he an' I got a special relationship, I guess you could say. Now, if you'll excuse me, I do have chores aroun' here t' take care of," and with that she stood once again, this time leaving the room completely.

Tori watched the man across the table from her as he played with his fork and empty plate. "You're quiet today," she mumbled.

"Yeah," he heaved a deep sigh. "Kinda stuck in the past for a moment, I guess. She an' I grew up one county over from each other, in Alabama. Funny, she still has th' accent, too. I managed t' get rid o' mine, for the mos' part. Only shows up at odd times these days." He chuckled; at what, Tori wasn't sure.

"You don't think you have an accent?" she teased.

He laughed louder, "Well, maybe I do an' I jus' don' hear it anymore."

Continuing to consume the delicious meal, she was surprised to see Mark Holt come barging into the room a few minutes later. Startled, she demanded, "Hey Mark, what're you doing here?"

"Beautiful morning," he grinned ear to ear. "I have some

fantastic news, and I wanted to wait until it was official before I shared any of it." Holding his hands out, palms up in dismay, he inquired, "Where's the guys?"

"Still sleeping, of course," she replied calmly, "Is it the kind of news we need to get them up for, or can it wait? They don't really like missing out on their beauty rest."

"Beauty rest," he laughed out loud, "Yeah, can't interrupt that, can we?" He paused, pursing his lips, then sputtered, "Ok, yeah let's wake them. We need to get moving," and he darted out the door and up the stairs to rouse the rest of his employers.

"Whatdaya suppose that's all about?" Brett asked absently.

"I have no idea. Pretty cryptic actually," she finished her plate hurriedly and moved to clean up her mess.

Minutes later, the rest of the men in the house found their way into the kitchen, including Enrique, all in various states of dress and demeanor. Once all the plates had been served, and everyone had established a location for consuming their portion, Mark excitedly called for their attention.

"I know you are all probably wondering why I have disturbed you on this glorious first day of the year," he began with an exaggerated preamble, "But I got the official word only an hour ago, and we need to get moving today."

Cody, ever in charge of speaking his mind, grumbled, "Well damn, Mark, we're all still half asleep or hung-over, so either spit it out or shut the fuck up." Leaning over his plate, holding his head, he obviously fell into the second of the two categories he had mentioned.

"Yes, well, I understand, but we have to get you guys on the plane," Mark explained further with a superlative wave of his hands, "As I said, it's official. Between Tori's interview on the show and the media blitz, you guys have been invited back to LA to finish the promo there, and there have been a few other stops added as well." He grinned at the girl, hoping that his pleasure at the turn of events more than evident.

Tori's head shot up at the mention of her previous residence, "They want us in LA?" she inquired timidly.

"Yes, tomorrow morning, in fact. We're going to complete the promo, and you are going to give a small private concert there in Terry's shop. He already started to prepare the raffle – only fifty people will win tickets to the event. Plus a few select reporters, and," he paused for effect, "There is talk of re-extending the tour. Some of the locations that backed out are having second thoughts about acting too hastily."

Tori could see her husband shift at the news, watching him with her peripheral vision as they were still not officially back on speaking terms. "That's great news!" she forced her lips into a smile, not sure that she liked the idea of being back so close to her old friends after Mason Hunt's visit.

The rest of the guys seemed far more enthusiastic, as even Cody managed a whoop, ringing ears, and all. Once the commotion had died down, and breakfast had all been put away, the group made their way upstairs to pack.

Knowing his sister and brother-in-law always travelled light, and as it turned out the two remaining Scorpions did as well, Brian made sure enough suitcases were produced out of storage for all. Taking hers to her room without argument, Tori began to pack her jeans, some light tees, and tank tops, well aware that the climate in California would be a stark contrast to that which they were currently experiencing.

She had only half finished when Michael joined her, hoisting his oversized pack onto the bed and flipping it open. Placing his hands on his hips, he stared at the scene, shaking his head in disgust. "Well, this is another fine surprise," he commented in a quiet voice, waiting to see if his bride would respond.

Cutting her eyes over at him, Tori could tell he wasn't actually pleased about the turn of events. Declining to comment, she allowed their disagreement to simmer, and returned to the closet to rummage for more clothes when she had a wickedly wonderful idea. Reaching for the bag that contained the leather mini and fishnet stockings, she pulled them out and carried them into the bedroom, waving them around for effect.

"I think I may give these a try while we're there, since the temperature will be more suited for them," she grinned at him with a wide-eyed stare and waited for the show.

Clenching his jaw, Michael had forgotten about most of the gifts his brother-in-law had presented to her on Christmas morning. Seeing the items brought the memory rushing to the surface, and he realized he probably should have removed them from the house completely if he actually wanted to prevent her from ever wearing them.

"Looks like you already have," he allowed the comment to fall flat across the clutter, and she quickly rolled up the stockings to avoid explaining in too much detail.

"Only to try them on," she cut her eyes over at him, her pulse thumping loudly in her ears, "I would have asked for your opinion, but I was afraid it would turn out like the swimsuit incident."

Michael could feel his face flush at the thought of what had occurred in Florida only a few short weeks before, "I apologized for that. I really didn't mean -" he stopped to regroup. "I bet you look real nice in them. Or something like that," his mind clouded at the image of her tall frame in the outfit and the attention she would get wearing it. His face drawn, he moved to the closet to begin packing his own gear for the trip.

Pursing her lips, Tori went to locate the matching boots and jewelry, the girl considered how having her mate around

126

was like always throwing a wet blanket on the fire. *He never enjoys the fun, and always finds a way to bring me down.* Refusing to continue the debate, she kept the rest of her attire hidden as she tucked it away and zipped up the suitcase, "Ok, I'm all set. I'll take this downstairs, and I'm ready to go."

"Yeah, I'm right behind you," he smiled, a feeble attempt to make peace.

Hauling the large satchel off the bed, Tori discovered that it had wheels, and she could roll it to the staircase before lifting for the short descent. Placing it next to the front door, she could see that only half of them were ready, and it occurred to her that it was a good thing the group always traveled by limo, as the car could seat ten people comfortably.

To her surprise, Enrique made his way up behind her, startling her when his hand grazed her hip. Half spinning, she came face to face with him to discover that he had cut his hair and trimmed his beard, "Jesus Christ, you scared the shit out of me!"

"Did I?" he chuckled, "Why's that? Do I remind you of someone?"

"No, you look like you," she found her herself smiling, lost in the past for a moment, "More like the first time we were in LA together, back at the halfway house." He only grinned, and she raised her hand to rest it against his chest, noting that it was covered in one of the new wife beaters that they had bought for him a few days before.

"You look real nice, baby," she added with a generous nod as he pulled on the button-down shirt that went over it, before she snapped herself back to the present and stepped back to avoid kissing him.

"Thanks," he gave her his best smile, sensing her softened emotions and catching his pet name again. Giving a quick glance around to ensure that they were alone, he sidled back up to her, closing the distance that she had put between them, "Listen... uh," he fiddled with the cuffs of his shirt until she took over the buttoning, "Thanks." His eyes flitted to hers, and he cleared his throat, "If you ever need anything... don't be afraid to ask. I'll always be here for you. Anything, anytime."

Tori looked up from the material she grasped to find his brown orbs were gazing at her attentively. Drawn in for a moment, she leaned slightly towards him and breathed a soft reply, "I know, baby. I won't forget."

Her tense smile small, he felt tempted to kiss her before he let her go with a wide grin, and adjusted his collar as he moved away. Finding a mirror in the right hand living area, he ran his fingers through what remained of his hair, "You don't thinks I took too much off?" he asked in a crisp voice.

"No," she replied instantly, "It's perfect. I like that buzzed look. It really suits you." Noticing Brett coming down the stairs she broke the connection reluctantly by calling out to the other man, "Ain't that right, Brett?"

"Ain't what right?" he countered playfully, not sure what he had missed.

"I said that the buzz cut looks good on him, don't you agree?"

"Pfft, it's a cut," the older man shook his red curls, "Like mine th' way it is. Only get it cut once or twice a year."

At that point, the conversation shifted to more serious matters, as the rest of the crew assembled and bags were placed in the limo. Climbing inside the car, there had been more than enough room for the group of eight, but Tori took a seat between the two Scorpions, forcing her husband to sit alone in their usual spot. She could feel him studying her, and she made it a point to make idle conversation with the two men for the rest of the ride for spite.

Upon boarding the group's private plane, things were

going to be a bit more cramped as there were eight passengers, and only eight seats, with no room to spare. Approaching the steps, Michael decided to be proactive in the matter, grasping his wife's arm firmly and pulling her closer as he hissed German in her ear, "You are going to sit next to me, right?"

A small grin curled her lips; she at least had the satisfaction of knowing that it bothered him somewhat that she had snubbed him. *Guess he isn't ready to hand me over to someone else yet after all.* "Sure, I can sit by you if you can behave yourself."

Michael's mouth flew open for a moment, and he caught himself before he said anything he would regret, "I'm sorry what I said upset you, ok? I didn't mean it that way. I want you to be happy; that's all. Why you gotta twist everything I say?"

Her eyes flicked down to his lips, "Why you always gotta make it sound like I'm the bad guy? Why is it always *me* doing the twisting?"

"Ugh," he made a noise as the wind escaped his lungs in a rush. "You know what," he chopped the air with a stiff hand, "You're unbelievable. On second thought, I'll sit by Mark, and you and your boyfriend can have a good time." Pushing past her, he made his way up the steps, choosing to let her stew.

Enrique had been standing close enough to pick up on the gist of the conversation, even if he didn't speak the language. "Lover's quarrel?" he teased her gently.

"Don't you start," she frowned at him, shoving a finger in his face.

Catching her hand, he only smiled as he leaned close enough to nuzzle her cheek with his nose, "He thinks we're sleeping together, don't he."

Giving him a bit of a shove, she nodded, "He knows that

we were close. And acting like this isn't helping the matter." She cast her eyes around the group, becoming aware that everyone was, in fact, watching them. "They all do, don't they. Think that we're fucking."

"It's in your nature," he replied with a half shrug, "Not that it bothers me for them to think so." He nuzzled her face again, and for an instant she thought he might kiss her.

"Stop that!" she commanded, a little too loudly before ratcheting her tone down. "We're not sleeping together, and you can get that thought out of your head right the fuck now." She punched him in the chest, "We're friends, end of story."

"Sure, baby girl," he laughed out loud as he rubbed the spot she had assaulted, "Whatever you say," his mind turning, convinced it was only a matter of time before he had her bent over a piece of furniture, and things were like old times, no matter how forcefully she denied it.

Make the Effort

Brian watched his sister as she flirted with the man next to her for nearly the full five-hour flight. Stealing glances at his brother-in-law, he felt a little putout that she would choose the thug over Michael. At least his brother-in-law had some sense about him, but this other guy was obviously a player. Deciding he and his sibling needed to have a talk, and soon, Brian relaxed into the seat and stared out the window in disgust.

Arriving in LA, the group took another limo to the luxury hotel where they would be staying, and the room assignments were given out. Enrique appeared to be somewhat disappointed that he and Brett were directed to share, and they were placed next door to Tori and Michael's suite, a double loss in his book. Watching as Michael helped his wife get her bag, he couldn't keep the jealousy off his face.

"You know you're goin' about this all wrong," Brett reprimanded as he opened their door.

"How you figure?" Enrique didn't budge, the couple's door practically closing in his face.

"I tol' you before, if you want 'er, you need t' be discrete. Out in th' open, she flirts with you, but she ain't goin' any further than that. She's havin' fun, and this ain't like bein' in th' crew. Different rules here." Enrique followed him into the room and closed the door.

"So you're saying I should act like I'm not interested in her? Kinda defeats the purpose, don't ya thinks?"

"No, man, you want 'er t' know, you jus' don' wan' everyone else t' know. She's married," he paused, giving the man an up and down look. "You wanna steal her away or be a fling?"

Enrique laughed, "That's a hells of a question."

"Hey, I'm not th' one who tol' her ol' man t' his face that I'd fuck 'er if I got the chance. Funny thing is, you two seem pretty cozy, an' he don' look too concerned about it, almost like he's lookin' the other way… on purpose. In the end, I don' think he cares if you do." Brett gave him an evil grin, "Cause in the end, all you got was a piece o' ass. He still gets t' keep the girl."

Enrique looked surprised, the truth in his words hitting home, "So you're sayin' he don't care if I'm bangin' his wife. Cause afterwards, he still owns her. Kinda like Eddie, sharin' his prize."

"Exactly," Brett raised his brow, nodding slightly. "Question is, are you happy with that, and will she be happy with that? Otherwise, we need to stay focused on what we're here to do, and that's to keep her safe. Leave the dickin' around to the pair o' them."

Tori stepped into the suite and took a look around, home sweet home for the next few weeks, maybe until the time came to make her trip to Texas. The thought of her doctor's appointment gave her a stab of guilt over her behavior on the plane, and she looked over at her husband curiously as he placed their things about the room.

"You know, it really isn't any fun if you don't care," she stated out of the blue.

"What isn't any fun?" he kept busy and didn't look her way.

"Enrique," she huffed noisily, "On the plane you were ignoring us." She hated the discovery touching him wasn't nearly as exciting without the thrill of getting caught.

"So?" he shrugged, "I'm not a kid, Tori. I told you to do what you wanted to do. I'm sorry if that spoils the fun for you, but I'm too old to play those kinds of games."

"And that's it. You *really don't care*," she shrugged her shoulders as she spoke, emphasizing the words. "I can go off and fuck whoever the hell I want, and you're gonna just look the other way," she flung her hand out into the room, indicating her meaning. "Just pretend it's not happening."

"But you won't do that," he stated confidently. "You don't want just anyone; you want him. And yes, I'm ok with that. I would prefer if you were a little more discrete about it. You know kissing and hanging all over him out in public is going to attract attention, but in the end, it is what it is. I knew that about you when I married you… that it would be a possibility that you would never get over it, but I was willing to take the chance. And I'm willing to live with that choice."

"What's that supposed to mean? Are you calling me a filthy whore and trying to be nice about it?" her eyes squinted in disgust.

He stopped what he was doing and glared at her. "I'm not calling you anything. I'm saying you don't change who you are without work. You lived that life for a long time, that role of being passed from man to man. If you're going to be someone else, it's you who will make the choice and you who will make the effort."

Tori stared at him, struck speechless for a moment. "You know, conversations with you have been pretty fucking pointless lately. I always come away from them feeling like I either got a lecture or some other kind of reprimand. I don't need you to tell me who and what I am. I got that covered." Resisting the urge to become physically violent, she turned her back on him with a grunt and stormed out of the room, slamming the door heavily behind her.

Out in the hall, she stomped to the elevator and pushed the button to the ground floor. Clenching her fists as she made her way out to the pool, she found an unoccupied lounge and dragged it over to an empty corner. The shade covered the spot nicely, and she wore an angry pout as she glanced around, wanting to be left alone. Flopping down on the bands of plastic, she curled her knees to her chest and stared blankly across the glistening water, her thoughts in turmoil as she considered the two men who were tearing her apart.

Tori felt a little surprised, and yet relieved that no one came looking for her. She stayed there for over an hour, only making her way inside when her stomach began to growl, and she had become calm enough to do something about it. Trudging into the dining room, she discovered the group of men already enjoying their dinner, and she felt reminded of the first night of her induction, when she stood before Eddie after she had disobeyed him and paid the price in flesh.

Keeping her face down, she took a seat in the only empty chair, between Cody and Collin and facing her husband. She was confronted almost immediately by the waiter, who seemed a little distraught that she had not been present when the rest of the orders were placed. Quickly opting for a steak with vegetables and a salad, she gave the man a weak smile, "And a glass of ice water, please."

The group talked pleasantly around her, and for a moment she wondered if they had agreed to ignore her, until she caught her husband's eye, and he smiled. Continuing with his meal, he glanced her way often, and she began to feel a small nest of hornets buzzing around in her belly. She wasn't sure what his expression had been meant to convey, based on their last conversation.

As soon as the others were finished eating, they broke up to go their separate ways. The plan was to meet in the lobby at 10:00 am the following morning to make their way over to the music store and on to a few other stops from there.

To her dismay, Brett and Enrique also left her. She scowled inwardly to herself at the knowledge that they weren't much protection if they didn't stay with her, and wondered if that was really why they were there. Chewing her meat slowly, she continued to contemplate the reasons that no one, besides the waiter, had spoken to her since she sat down.

As she finished cleaning her plate, Michael moved around next to her, leaning back in the chair and taking her in. "You ok?"

"Yeah," she shrugged. "Needed some time to think, that's all."

He reached over, toying with a few strands of dark hair that covered her ear. Using the same finger, he waved it over at the dance floor, where the band had begun to play, "Would you like to dance?"

"To that shit?" she mocked the music that wafted across the room, "I don't even know what the hell that is!"

"It's called a waltz," he laughed quietly. Standing, he offered her his hand, "Come on, I'll show you."

Looking up at him, she puckered her lips, not sure she wanted to accept. "Is it hard?" she could feel the color rising in her cheeks, recalling that she had never actually danced with a partner before, unless leaning against Enrique and rocking back and forth counted.

"Naw, it only takes a little practice," he curled his digits to entice her.

Reaching up, she slid her fingers into his, mildly

surprised that he would want to be close to her after the way she had behaved. Their palms mingling as they moved through the tables, he guided her towards the parquet floor, then turned to face her and positioned their hands. Giving her a brief explanation of the steps, he smiled and ended by commanding her to relax and follow his lead.

Tori did her best, and he praised her often as she moved her body in sync with his, "You're doing great, baby girl. That's it, look me in the eye."

She smiled at the tenderness of his voice, "You're really better than I deserve, you know that?" His hand moved against her waist, causing her brain to go fuzzy.

"Deserve's got nothing to do with it, love… focus," but he squeezed her hand and grinned at the same time.

His body pressed against hers, she could feel the tickle as his hand caressed her back beneath her long tresses. His cheek often moved close to hers, his warm breath sending shivers down her spine, and it surprised her that as long as they had been together, he could still make her weak in the knees with a simple touch. Adjusting her fingers inside of his grasp, she wondered if he would always have that effect on her.

The couple twirled around the floor for over an hour, stopping a few times to have a drink of water and refresh. Each time, he would give her compliments on what she did well, and pointers where she could improve, and she took each lesson in stride, finding herself eager to please him.

Eventually, they made their way to the elevator, where Tori leaned against the mirror in the back and stared at her mate. "Why do you put up with me?"

He laughed at her silly question, "You know, someday, you're going to figure out that I've been telling you the truth all along. We each have a half that makes them a whole, and you're mine. It's that simple."

Grinning, she pulled herself up straight so she could wrap her arms around him as if an evening on the dance floor hadn't been enough. Leaning her forehead against the hair above his ear, she exhaled warm puffs against the curved cartilage, "Make love to me tonight?"

Looping an arm around her, "You won't have to ask me twice," he replied.

Talking quietly as they made their way down the hall, the couple slipped inside the room and turned on a few lights. Taking it slow, they removed their boots and stretched out on the over-sized bed for a bit of petting; eventually removing her shirt and pants. Michael made sure he gave her all that he had to offer, confident in the end that she belonged to him, no matter what anyone else might have believed.

How the Other Half Died

Things were hectic the following morning, and the group piled into the car to make their way over to the Music Maniac to meet with Terry. Tori found her palms were sweaty at the idea of returning to the store, and she briefly wondered if any of the guys still worked there.

She had grown particularly fond of Max, and of the three young men, he was the one she would be most interested in seeing again. Arriving at their destination, her questions were answered right away as all three of them were waiting for the group to arrive.

"Oh, my God, look who's here!" she squealed, holding her arms above her head as she raced towards her favorite and grabbed him first. However, not to be impolite, she hugged the other two as well, and for a moment it seemed like she had never left.

"This is incredible!" Derrick congratulated her, "I can't believe you're actually playing in a band!"

"Well, since I never let on that I could play, I guess that's understandable," she grinned at her young friend, noting his attempt at growing a beard, "You look rather handsome, by the way. I like the..." she rubbed the back of her fingers against her chin to indicate what she referred to, and he laughed.

"Yeah, it's still pretty scraggly, but I'm sure it will fill in if I give it time." His eyes sparkled as he stared, "It really is great to see you."

"Alright, knock it off," Terry came over to send the three back to work. "Hi, baby girl," he took the young woman in his arms himself and gave her a firm squeeze. "I have a message. Sharon Tate says that if you don't at least make time for a lunch date, she's disowning you."

Tori laughed out loud, "Oh, she did? Well, I guess I need to find out what day that can be arranged and give her a call."

"Yeah, that sounds like a good idea. Hello, Mike," turning to her husband he shook his hand, and they exchanged pleasantries before he made his way around to the rest of the group, being introduced to Brett and Enrique as well. If he were surprised that their number had grown, he never let on, and a short time later everything had been determined, and they were off to the next stop.

Back inside the car, Tori called out to their manager, "Hey Mark, what time will I be free for a girl's day out with my friend?"

He nodded slightly, and pursed his lips, "Our schedule is actually pretty tight since you've requested to be off starting the first of February, but we do have twenty-nine days that we are looking at here, so I'm sure we can squeeze in a lunch date somewhere in there."

"Thanks, hun; you're the best," she grinned at the thought of having a little time to catch up with her old friend.

Arriving at the studio a short time later, they went in to take care of making some spots for radio stations to use across the country, and Tori found that she had grown very relaxed in the company of the group. Anything she didn't understand, they readily explained; all she had to do was ask. It turned out to be an exciting, and maybe even pleasant afternoon, as far as she was concerned.

For the three men looking after her, the day seemed a bit more stressful. The group pulled up in front of the studio and made their way inside. Standing next to the car during the process, Enrique caught a glimpse of a familiar face before it vanished around the corner of the building, "Wow, that's disturbing," he muttered to himself as the dark haired man disappeared.

Glancing around at the rest of the group, he slapped Michael's arm, "Hey, mind if I hangs around down here for a bit? You know, whiles the rest of you go up and take care of business." The other man appeared lost in thought, staring at the same corner Enrique had been interested in. "Hello, Earth to Mike," he waved his hand in front of his face.

Snapping back to reality, Michael glanced around to find that the rest of the group had moved on without them, and the two of them stood in front of the building alone, "What? Where'd everyone go?"

"Upstairs." Enrique squinted at the corner, "You saw him too, didn't you."

"Saw who?" Michael tried to play it off, surprised that Enrique would know anything about Eli Founder.

"I dunno his name. Some federal guy; gave me some grief here a whiles back." He paused as he recalled that the man had actually ordered him to kill the one standing next to him. His brow furrowed, he probed, "You got some kinda beef with that guy? I don't think he likes you very much."

Michael cut his eyes over at him, considering his words carefully to form a reply, "I married his girl. So yeah, we don't like each other very much." He looked around on the street another half a minute, "I think we should follow him, see if we can find where he went. What he's doing here. I don't think it's a coincidence that he's this close to us."

Enrique grinned, "Sure thing. But if we follow him, he'll run and hide. We need to set a trap. Between the two of us, if he's up to no good, we'll get him."

"Agreed. If he's tailing us, we can be on the lookout, catch him when he's not expecting it. Let's head upstairs, check on the others."

Locating the group and making sure that all was well, Michael briefed Brett in private about the tail. Giving him a quick rundown on their plan to catch the guy, the older man gave him a surprised look before agreeing to keep an eye on the group so the other two could see if they could find him.

Back downstairs, the pair took a secondary exit out of the building, hoping to catch Eli with his pants down, so to speak. Spying a coffee shop across the street, Michael grinned, "I bet he's in there. Perfect place to hide. You hang out here by the exit, and I'll go in to confront him. If he comes out, don't be seen, but follow him. If he don't come out, you can come in and join us."

"Got it," Enrique nodded, putting on his game face.

Michael strode over and pulled on the glass door, removing his dark glasses as he entered. His eyes quickly scanned the patrons, and sure enough, he found the one he wanted.

Eli sat in the corner next to the window, pretending to read a magazine and watching the front of the studio. Walking straight up to him, he slid into the booth next to his target to prevent him from leaving, "Hello, Eli; long time, no see."

Stunned, Eli shut the set of glossy pages, almost dropping it in his lap, "Mike Anderson, what the hell are you doing here?"

"What am I doing here?" he pointed his hand at his chest. "Whatever the fuck I feel like. What I wanna know is why you're following us," Michael demanded, deciding to get right to the point.

"Following you? What makes you think I'm following

you?" he stammered at being caught. "Oh great, and what are you doing here?" he addressed Enrique as he moved into the seat across the table from him.

"Enrique, this is Eli. Special Agent Founder as a matter of fact. He's been on Tori's case since the beginning." Michael pointed his finger at the other man as he spoke.

"Oh, thanks, Mike; nice to put a name with a face. So, got any more missions for me lately?" Enrique taunted the other man. "Oh, I guess not. I haven't heard from you in a while, so I guess you're all done with me."

Eli clenched his jaw, trying not to panic as the anger brewed beneath the surface, "Look, I have no idea what you guys are up to, but I'm here on official business and you two clowns are interfering. If you don't get out of my way, I'm going to arrest you for obstruction of justice."

"Arrest us?" Michael sneered with a chuckle. "We're having lunch, man. We saw you and thought we'd join you. Of course, if you want to tell us what's really going on, we would be more than happy to get out of your way."

"Yeah," Enrique tossed in. "Or we could drag you out back and beat it out of you."

Michael stared at the other man in a state of mock shock. "Hey! We're not here to torture the guy. I'm sure he's gonna tell us everything, aren't ya, Eli?" Michael grinned at the man next to him, laying his arm on the back of the booth behind him so he could bump the back of his head periodically.

"I don't know what kind of game you're playing, but I'm a federal officer. Touching me is assault —"

"Oh yeah?" Michael moved his hand, tagging him firmly, "I don't think we're scared of that, Eli. Maybe you should call your friends, get some help in here."

Eli's blue eyes glared at him coldly, "You really are an asshole, you know that?"

"Yeah, I am," he wacked him a little harder. "Oops, sorry about that. Maybe you should start talking before I'm forced to give in to my friend's request and haul you outside."

"Ok, I'm following her, ok?" Eli smoothed his hair. "One of our agents was killed, and I want to make sure nothing happens to her. For a few weeks, until we know that things are taken care of," he kept his cool, spitting out the lie without blinking.

"Agent? What agent? It wasn't that jerk off, La Buff was it?"

"No, it wasn't him. It was someone else, who may or may not have had connections to her case. That's why I'm worried. You know that I care about her, and I sure as hell don't want to see anything happen to her. So why don't you go back where you belong and let me handle this? Before you get me in trouble..." his voice trailed away as he finished his plea.

Michael shifted, muttering under his breath, "Just 'cause you fucked her don't mean that you care, dickwad." Staring out the window, he wanted a moment to think.

Enrique started to laugh, "You knows, last time we met, you talked down to me like I was shit. Now you seems nervous as hell. How do we know you ain't lyin' to us?"

"You're going to have to trust me," Eli indicated the man seated next to him. "Mike knows. Knows I wouldn't put her in harm's way."

Michael snorted, "I don't know anything of the sort. But I do know this: if anything does happen to her, you'll be the first person I come after." Standing abruptly, he headed for the door, Enrique hot on his heels.

"You think that was the truth?"

"Don't matter, we scared him, and that's enough. We watch more closely though; for him, for anyone else who looks like a Fed, and for anything out of the ordinary."

Enrique swung around nervously, feeling like a caged animal now that he was aware they were being watched. "You gonna tell her?"

"No. We can't do anything about it at this point, and she don't need to know," he cut his eyes over at the other man. "And you're not gonna tell her either, ya got it?"

"Sure, man. I won't say nothing. We gotta tells Brett though, so he can help us keep an eye out. Damn, looks like he was right, too."

"Who, Brett?" Michael asked as he punched the button inside the elevator.

"Yeah, Brett. He said The Organization would come for her. If the Feds are watching her, it may happen pretty soon."

"Yeah," Michael agreed. "I bet we don't have to wait long."

Arriving back in the lobby area, where Brett and Mark were seated, Michael pulled the red-headed man aside to fill him in on what they had discovered. Brett quickly agreed they should keep an eye out, and they looked around to find some coffee while they waited for the taping to be completed.

Memory Lane

A few days into their hectic schedule, the band received a small break in the form of a dinner invitation at the half-way house. Tori felt ecstatic to accept the request, and it was arranged for them to spend a few hours there with the Tates.

Pulling up in front of the massive structure, she could feel her fingers tingle, and clenched them into fists repeatedly, a small grin curling her lips. As the seven of them exited the vehicle, Michael reached to take her hand, and she gladly curled her fingers into his, ready to present her spouse to her surrogate parents in the first real home she could remember.

Giving a quick knock and making her way into the kitchen through the back door, Tori inhaled deeply, the sight and smell of the place magically transporting her back in time. Finding the mistress of the property alone in the kitchen, preparing their meal, Tori gave her friend a small wave hello and urged the guys to move inside.

Sharon came forward to welcome her guests, hoping the girl who had touched her heart so deeply would be receptive to a hug. Meeting her in front of the bar, the taller woman clung to her friend, pangs of regret at not keeping in touch wriggling into her gut.

After a lengthy embrace, Sharon explained that the

current residents had relinquished the house for the evening, and they had some other guests who would be joining them. "Your room is currently vacant if you want to have a peek, for old time's sake. We'll set the table and wait for the others."

Tori smiled at the surprise, and wondered who the mystery participants would be, "Haha, you know I'd love to have a look around. You sure you don't need any help down here?"

"No, ma'am; you go make yourself at home. We'll call you when we're all set down here," Sharon gave her a squeeze on the arm, a bit concerned at the tiredness the young woman's makeup didn't cover.

Casting a quick glance around, Tori excused herself from the group of men, who were busy making themselves glasses of soda and iced tea, the snickers at the selection audible. Heading up the stairs, she laughed at their amazement. *It's a half-way house after all; surely they didn't expect to be served alcohol.* Her foot reaching the landing, she froze, the air hanging in her chest at the sight of the two portals to the rooms at her left.

Her digits resting on the corner post, she recalled the morning Enrique had pressed her against the wall between the two doors, placing his hand beneath her towel and staking his claim. *So much has happened since then.* She blinked at the space as the moment of recognition replayed in her mind, and the fear it had brought crashing in around her.

Moving into her old quarters, she exhaled a deep sigh, *nothing to fear these days. Enrique watches over me, as does, Brett, Michael and the rest of our little group.* Making it to the window, she propped her right knee onto the seat, placing her palms on the glass and peering down at the storage building below her. Still visible in the fading light of evening, recalling the excitement of the treasure she had found inside it widened her grin.

Feeling a hand grasping at her waist, Tori jumped, "What the fuck?" Spinning around with a jerky movement, she put her foot back on the floor, facing the intruder. Her pulse pounded in her ears for a moment from the jolt and anger at having been interrupted.

"Sorry, baby girl; didn't means t' startle you," Enrique's brown orbs danced as he pushed the hand around to her back, drawing her against him.

"What're you doing up here?" she managed, gasping for breath, her hand shoved against his chest to keep him at bay.

His palm moved up and down her spine, "Oh, enjoying the trip down memory lane, alongs with you, I guess. I never made it into this room back then." He flashed his pearly whites, eyes darting around the small space. Leaning forward slightly, he kept his voice low, "Those was good times for me." His nose nuzzled her cheek, and she felt the shivers the air brushing against it unleashed.

Her hand finding its way up from his chest to his neck, she caressed his mandible with her thumb, enjoying the tickle of his short beard beneath it. "Yeah, it wasn't so bad, was it?" The two of them rocking side to side slightly, he placed his forehead against hers.

"You knows," his voice steady, "I always wished I'd taken you with me that night… when I left you in the bar."

"Don't, baby," she pushed her palm to rest where her fingers had been exploring on his jaw, "We can't change the past."

His hand found the back of hers and pressed it against his skin, sliding it to touch it to his lips. "I know," he breathed, massaging her flesh, then shifting to place his mouth over hers.

The kiss electric, it sent sparks of excitement through her, and she broke the connection briefly before parting her lips and taking him in while pushing the full front of herself against him. Lost in the moment, she became distantly aware of the knock on the door frame as it interrupted her thoughts, forcing a wedge into her clouded mind.

"Guys," Brian's voice sounded irritated, "Dinner's ready," he repeated for the third time. His eyes met hers for an instant, and he shook his head in disgust before turning his back and making his way back down the stairs.

Enrique chuckled, "Sorry, baby girl; I'm sures you'd rather he hadn't seen that," and he released her reluctantly.

Tori ran her hands over her clothing, smoothing it and her nerves simultaneously, "It's ok. Only a kiss after all." But she grinned, the thrill of being close to him overwhelming her for a moment. *I wonder if he knows that Michael doesn't care about... us.* Leaning forward, she pressed her lips to his once more for another quick taste, sighing when she pulled back to lead the way.

Arriving in the kitchen, Tori noticed that Brandon had joined them and was giving Enrique a hard stare when he followed her into the room. "Oh, my," she laughed. "I forgot that he stayed here for a bit and that you guys had met."

"Yes, we've met," Brandon spoke in a begrudging tone. "I guess you two were closer than we realized."

"Just friends," Tori intervened before Enrique could reveal any details into their relationship. Reaching to reclaim her mate's hand, "I guess you met my husband, Michael," her voice softened as she announced him. She forced a smile through the twinge of guilt, wondering how many of them had guessed what she and Enrique had been doing upstairs.

His attention diverted, the house manager gave him a nod; "Yes, we've all been introduced." His eyes briefly flicking between the two men, he let the subject drop as Tori was a grown woman, and capable of making her own decisions.

Serving plates of steaks and steamed vegetables, Tori felt overjoyed to see that they had remembered her diet. Taking a seat next to Sharon, the two women chitchatted about how things were going, until they were interrupted by a knock on the door and Jonathon let himself in.

Seeing the young man brought Tori another wave of memories, including the first trip to the AA meeting and the talks that the two of them had shared as she made her recovery. Standing from her seat, she welcomed him with a warm hug, and he seemed eager to hear about what currently went on in her life. Finally, he would be able to meet her family and new friends, and she happily introduced them, proud of who they were and how much they meant to her.

The group remained at the table, enjoying beverages and conversation after the meal, until the doorbell rang at the front of the house. Moving to the living area, they caught the door as they made their way down the hall, and Tori let loose with a loud squeal, pouncing on the girl who stood in the doorframe and screaming, "Oh my God, you came!"

A little surprised by her reaction, Lindsey recognized the show of emotion as undoubtedly the greatest she had ever seen from her. The tall young woman could easily be called one of her best friends, and she replied with a loud giggle, "Of course I came, silly. Did you really think I would miss it?"

Clinging to the petite blond and trying to avoid injuring her in her excitement, Tori presented her to the group, "Guys, this is Lins. She is absolutely my best female friend ever."

Michael grinned broadly as he offered his hand, finding it amusing that his bride still categorized her friendships as male and female, knowing that the male version outnumbered the female by a landslide. Pushing the thought aside, he moved with the rest, who spread out in the large living area and broke up into smaller units of conversation.

The pair of girls climbed into the window seat on the front wall, where Tori eagerly plied her young friend with questions, and discovered that she had begun taking some college courses the previous fall. "Classes start back next week, and I'm looking forward to getting back into the routine," Lins shared as the two girls began to chatter.

"Is it hard?" Tori pressed her, still unsure about how education worked in a classroom setting.

"Naw, not really," her friend shook her golden waves, noticing that Brian had become quite fascinated with their exchange, "It's time-consuming more like." Tilting her head and placing her hand along her face to hide her lips, she indicated the guy who stared her down, "He's your brother, right?"

"Yeah," Tori giggled. "He has a thing for short blond girls. Plus, he's a bit over protective of me, I think," she gave him a grin as she spoke, noticing that the girl flushed at the situation. "Don't worry, he's pretty harmless."

"That's good," her friend teased. "I'm avoiding those kinds of entanglements for the time being. I want to finish school and really be sure of who I am before I take that kind of step." She grinned, her green eyes sparkling, "I'm not sure things would have worked out this way for me... you know... if you hadn't been here."

Tori shrugged, giving herself a minute to formulate her response, "I sometimes think the same thing about you. I learned so much from you about myself. Things I couldn't see before." Reaching over, she hugged the girl to her, blinking rapidly to avoid having her tears revealed. "Thanks for coming tonight."

By 11:00 pm, the two had had their fill, for the time being at least, and were ready to say their goodbyes. As the group exited the house, Brian seemed to have a small brainstorm, "Hey, sis; let's take Lins back to the hotel with us. That way, you guys can spend a few more hours catching up," and he gave the pretty blonde a wink as he made the suggestion.

Tori's jaw dropped slightly before she huffed, "That won't be necessary. Maybe she and I can meet for lunch before we're finished here, and she gave me her number, so we'll definitely keep in touch at any rate."

Hurrying the guys into the car, she hugged Sharon and Lins one last time, and joined them, sliding into the seat between Michael and Enrique while licking her upper lip anxiously. Brian could see that her mood had waned, and clenched his jaw in disgust.

"Why couldn't we bring her? She's cute," he demanded stiffly.

Shifting in her seat, Tori internally struggled with making her reply. She knew she didn't want to divulge too much of the girl's past. However, she needed to make it clear she wanted her brother to stay away from the girl. Rolling her eyes, she tried to keep it simple, "She's special, Danny. Like me. She had a really hard life, and she's doing well... she doesn't need to get involved with... us..." her voice trailed away, allowing the final word to hang in the air.

"What the hell is that supposed to mean?" he demanded curtly. "You make it sound like we're bad people or we would hurt her or somethin'. Or are you scared she would do something to me?" he eyed her suspiciously. "Did she say anything about me?"

"No, she didn't, Danny. I don't think it would be a good idea, that's all," she clenched her hands together nervously. "I know she's your type, but she really had a bad childhood. So bad, if she and I were in a contest for whose was worse, I'm not sure that I would win."

Her brother rolled his tongue, "And that matters... why?"

Tori ground her teeth, seeing that being diplomatic wasn't getting her anywhere, "Look, Danny, if you want to make me say it, then it matters because you're not good at relationships, and I want you to leave my friend alone. She don't need that shit."

Brian's eyes darted between his sister and the two men who flanked her, "I'm not good at relationships? When you're upstairs playing tonsil hockey with your boyfriend while your husband's back is turned?"

Tori's features froze in horror, having their private moment made public, in the middle of a fight no less. Her brow furrowed, she tossed her long curls; "That's not what happened."

Brian released a loud howl of laughter, "What the fuck do you mean *'that's not what happened'*?" he mocked her tone. "I know what I saw! What I've been seeing," his face contorted in anger.

"Enrique and I are just friends!" she interrupted, instantly regretting the outburst. She knew she protested too hard to be convincing, especially since she had, in fact, been kissing him.

"Just friends?" Brian scoffed. "Everyone sees the way you two are together; you can't deny that you're fucking him. And your old man lets it go on like it's no big deal," he tossed a thumb at the man on her right.

"Hey! I think this is getting a little personal," Michael cut in.

Brian sneered, "I'm only speaking the truth here, and if that's the way you guys wanna live, I'm great with that." He pointed his finger at his sister, "But don't you go trashing me and my life because you don't think I'm 'good at relationships.' You ain't any better."

Tori didn't respond, pissed beyond words. *Who the hell does he think he is?* She had denied that she and Enrique were lovers, but what would it matter? The point had gotten lost in the argument, and in the end, all she wanted was to protect her young friend from getting involved when it would prove fruitless in the end.

Sitting in silence, the group made it to the hotel and went their separate ways. Slamming the door to their room, Michael reached out and caught his wife's arm, "So, what did I miss upstairs?"

Tori stood staring at him, mouth hanging wide open in shock. He didn't back down, and it took her a minute to close it to respond, "Nothing. We were talking about old times, and he kissed me, right when Brian showed up to call us for dinner."

Michael's gaze dropped to watch her lips move as she spoke, his mind racing. He had told her he didn't care, and felt disgusted by his cross-examination. Shoving his hands in his pockets, he blew noisily out through his nostrils, "I warned you people were going to notice."

"I'm not sleeping with him!" her eyes flashed. "I swear to you, not since he's been here!"

He turned his back on her, moving to the window and placing his arm over his head as he peered out through the glass. "I'm sorry; I shouldn't have asked. I told you I didn't care, and I meant it. If you need him to be happy," he paused, his voice dropping, "If you need those things that he is willing to do for you…"

Tori's gut wrenched, her pulse bulging in her throat, "You don't believe me."

"I don't need to believe you. That's not the point. The point is, I shouldn't have asked." Turning enough to look at her, he could see the dazed expression on her face. "I'm sorry the evening ended on a bad note. I know you were really excited to see your friends."

"DON'T CHANGE THE SUBJECT," she bellowed.

"We're not finished with this conversation! I want you to understand. I want you to *believe* me."

Michael blinked at her, thoughts swirling, *nice move, asshole. What're you gonna do now, call her a liar to her face?* Dropping his arm, he reached for her, "Come here, love. I never said I don't believe you. I said it doesn't matter."

"It does fucking matter!" she punched him in the chest, stepping back out of his grasp. "What is it that you want, Michael? You *want* me to choose him?" She could feel the angry tears building.

"Not at all," he breathed a deep sigh, folding his arms behind his back. "I want you. All I have ever wanted... is you. I can't make it any plainer than that."

"Yeah, well, you got a funny way of showing it!" Tori spun around and yanked the door open, slamming it behind her. Wiping the streams from her cheeks, she stomped down the hall and entered the elevator. Pausing only for an instant, she punched the button, headed for the bar.

Angry All the Time

Son of a bitch, no wonder I'm fucking angry all the time. Taking a seat on a leather-covered stool, she waved at the barkeep, "I need a double shot of vodka."

"Yes ma'am," he replied crisply, fetching a glass and placing it in front her with a thud. Watching him pour, she could feel her mouth fill with saliva.

"On second thought, leave the bottle," she requested, anger still dripping from her voice, and he smiled, placing it next to the glass before he walked away.

Tori reached over, lifting the container to inspect the label. Setting it back on the bar, she released a heavy sigh, deep lines creasing her forehead. Pushing the glass back, she crossed her arms to rest her chin on them, staring at the liquid fire. *I don't understand men one damn bit.*

Almost immediately she realized that wasn't true. *I do know how to get them to take off their clothes, generally speaking.* She grinned to herself, imagining how easy it was to do, in fact. *And I know what to do after that.* Reaching over, she extended her index finger, allowing it to trace the rim of the glass. *Why am I fighting it? Why don't I simply have them both?*

I could, you know, she rationalized with herself, *neither of them seems too concerned about sharing. The only one*

155

who cares is me... Tori continued to allow her thoughts to turn, toying with her drink until her lids grew heavy, and she drifted off to sleep.

Awakened with a start, Tori opened her eyes. Sitting up straight, she rubbed her arms, which were stiff from the awkward position. "What time is it?" she asked the bartender, who stood in front of her, scowling.

"Time for you to leave, that's what time it is. You've been here for hours, and it's time to close up," he grabbed the shot and tossed it into the sink behind him. Lifting the bottle, he returned it to the shelf.

Tori stared at him, sliding off the stool, "Sorry," she mocked him with her tone, not really sure why he spoke to her so rudely. "Put the bottle and drink on my tab." Turning away, she groggily made it to the elevator and leaned against the wall while she waited for the shiny doors to part and let her inside.

Stumbling down the hall, she arrived back at her room a few minutes later. She didn't bother with the light, stripping down and climbing into the bed naked. Exhausted from the day filled with ups and downs, she dropped off to sleep almost immediately, not the least bit worried if the man next to her actually knew she had come back or not.

Tori awakened at 9:00 am the following morning, Michael's hand gripping her shoulder to shake her, "Hey," he said loudly, "Time to get up."

Covering her face with her arm to hold out the glare, she tumbled out of the sheets to comply, not surprised by the angry clip of his words, "We have another photo shoot this morning don't we."

"Yeah, and we're late," he tossed clothes on the bed for her. "I tried to let you sleep in, but Mark called, and they're waiting for us downstairs. Impatiently, I might add."

"You mean the guys beat me awake?" she grimaced as

she shoved her legs into the jeans before pulling them off. "I need a shower. They will have to wait."

"Then hurry. I'll go down and stall them," he offered, his eyes roaming up and down her naked curves.

Tori made her way into the bathroom, hearing the door close as she reached for the faucet. Washing her hair and body, she stepped out of the tub and threw on the clothes, smearing her makeup on her face and painting her eyes. Giving herself a once over in the full-length mirror, she frowned, wishing she could call in sick for the day.

A few minutes later, she joined the group of anxious men in the restaurant, taking her place at the table. "Hey guys," she managed weakly.

"Hey yourself," Cody tossed out bitterly. "Where the fuck have you been? We're fucking late, so hurry your ass up."

A plate of eggs and bacon was placed in front of her, which had been ordered for her to try and speed things along. Crinkling her nose as her stomach lurched, she shoved at the meal. "I'm not hungry. But I'll take some coffee," she muttered, and the waitress placed a cup of the black liquid before her.

Tori sipped the dark shot of caffeine while noticing that Michael and Enrique were each giving the other an angry glare. She briefly considered what the two of them were pissed off about, but didn't bother to ask.

As soon as the container was empty, Collin jumped up from his seat, "That's it, let's go."

"Jesus Christ, calm the fuck down! You act like no one has ever been late before!" she snapped, placing the cup on the table with a loud bang. Standing, she followed the rest of her bandmates to the car and slid into her usual spot since they had arrived in LA, with Enrique seated on her left and Michael on her right.

She frowned the entire ride, noticing that everyone seemed to be in a foul mood. Finally, when she couldn't take anymore, she tried to defend herself, "Ok, I'm sorry I was late. I was tired and needed some sleep," she stretched and gave a yawn for effect.

"This was important," her brother glared at her. "You know; we do our share of fucking around, but when it comes to business... you don't mess with that." His accusing eyes flicked between the two men, wondering which of them responsible for her exhaustion.

The group arrived at the studio a short while later, where the other bands from their upcoming tour were waiting for the photo shoot. Being introduced, Tori managed to shake hands with most of them, and they were put into their positions for the spread of shots. More than once, she gave wide, exaggerated yawns, and the photographer kept reminding her from time to time to focus or to smile, as she had a difficult time doing either.

Taking a break a few hours in, Mark pulled the girl to the side, "I thought you had sworn off alcohol," he demanded through clenched teeth.

Taken aback, Tori stammered, "I did!"

"Then why were you in the bar last night with a bottle of vodka, and why are you hung over this morning?"

"I'm not hung over!" she denied the charge, "And I never touched the glass. I stared at it; that's it. And who the hell told you I was there, anyways?"

Lips pursed; Mark flipped open a tabloid in front of her, her picture plastered across the front page, causing her to gasp loudly. "Holy shit, that was fast! Who the hell took the picture?!?" Her dark hair partially covered her face, but the bottle and glass sitting in front her passed out form told the story clearly.

"It doesn't matter," he bit angrily. "That's how it works

in showbiz. People take pictures and to get the scoop, they gotta move fast. You know what this says?" he slapped the page with his free hand.

"No," her doleful eyes stared at the image.

"It says you're a drunk! And then you show up here, looking like shit and moping around like you have one hell of a hangover," he clenched his jaw. "And it puts all the hard work I've done on your behalf in jeopardy."

Tori's gaze shifted, the words *looking like shit* ringing in her ears, she shouted, "Well, I don't feel fucking good today, and that ain't why!" she slapped the pages out of his hand and watched them scatter beneath her.

"What the hell is going on over here?" Michael interrupted them, and she noticed that the entire room was staring at them.

Shifting uncomfortably, she held up both hands in the form of surrender. Swallowing hard, she realized there wasn't any point in denying any of it; the evidence lay in black and white on the floor. "I need a break," she stated flatly and turned her back on the group, making her way to the door.

Climbing on the elevator, she cast a quick glance over her shoulder to see if anyone had followed her. Much to her relief, they hadn't, and she made her way downstairs easily enough. Locating the car, the driver sitting in the front seat reading a book, she knocked on the window, "I need to get inside," she spit out as calmly as she could muster.

"No problem, hop in," he smiled, tossing a thumb towards the back.

Opening the door and closing it with a heavy slam, Tori wriggled into the seat, laying her head back and breathing deeply. *If they gave awards for stupid moves, you could be a daily contender;* she cursed herself as she stared at the roof above her. Continuing to inhale and then exhale in a slow and steady rhythm, she could feel herself begin to relax, followed by a deep urge to crash.

A little nap, that's all I need, she rationalized as she lay over in the seat. Curling her legs up onto the leather covering, she rested her cheek on her hands, closed her eyes, and a few minutes later she was out cold.

Crazy Lifestyle

Tori awoke to find the rest of the group taking their places in the car around her. Sitting up on the seat, she stretched, mumbling her inquiry as to what was going on.

"We're done," Brian stated flatly. "Shoot's over. We finished without you." His expression bleak, he gave her an ominous ache in the pit of her stomach.

Scooting over next to her, Michael claimed her hand before reaching up to smooth the red marks left on her face from the seat, "Jesus, love, are you ok?"

"I'm fine. Really tired, that's all," she looked at him, aware that everyone stared at her once again. "So, it's ok? They weren't mad or anything?"

"They weren't happy, if that's what you mean," Mark quipped, "And how things will go remains to be seen. Suffice it to say, you get to rest tonight, and we pick up again tomorrow. Go to bed, get some fucking sleep. We still have a few weeks to repair the damage before you get your time off."

Tori inhaled sharply, trying to make sense of things as her thoughts seemed hazy at the moment. "And what happens after my break?"

"We get back to work. We still have a lot to do, and there is the private concert that will take place after you get back," he paused, rolling his tongue. "I don't have to tell you I'm disappointed in you. I think most everyone here is, at this point."

Tori flinched, ready to accept her reprimand.

"All we can do is go from here," he continued, pointing a stiffened finger at her. "That means that you have to be on your best behavior. No more late night escapades. No more hanging all over Enrique in public places. You're on the edge, and a shift in public opinion could send you over."

Tori nodded, "Yeah, I get it," she glanced at the man to her left, surprised they hadn't insisted that he leave. Inhaling deeply, she spoke in a low tone, "I'm really sorry about all of this." She made the apology, still not sure why it had all happened.

Over the course of the next week, Tori struggled with her exhaustion and took naps often to overcome it. She focused hard on doing what they asked of her, keeping her mouth shut most of the time to avoid the snide comments that seemed to fly out of nowhere whenever she spoke. She kept to herself most of the time as a last resort to combat the inner rage that had taken over her mind and spirit, as the least little thing would be enough to send her into a tirade.

Enrique and the others hardly spoke to her, keeping their distance in an effort to maintain the peace. His absence bothered her more than she wanted to let on, growing sullen and somewhat resentful that Michael was the only one who spent any real time with her.

He quickly became more like her jailer rather than her spouse, and she could feel their relationship deteriorating under the strain. A full seven days after the picture of her with a bottle of vodka hit the front page, she wasn't sure how much longer she could go on.

Deciding she needed to speak up, she called a meeting with the rest of the group, opting for the privacy of their suite. The group of men appeared tense, taking seats in chairs that formed a circle, reminding her of group sessions back in the hospital. Looking around calmly, she did her best to put their minds at ease. "Hey, guys; relax. It's only a rough spot," and she gave them her best smile to emphasize the point. "I'm feeling better, and that's a good sign."

"We're worried about you, baby girl," Enrique raised his chin as he spoke, the dark circles under his eyes evidence of his concern. "I've been staying away from you, but you don't really looks like it's helping."

Tori grinned, "It's helping, baby. Really it is." Biting her lip, she paused, "I guess what I wanted was to thank you all for your support and for your patience. I think you know this hasn't been easy for me. The stress here," she chuckled lightly, "Well, this's different from anything else I've ever done."

"That's all I can say as far as the reason. I'm just tired, and it puts me in a bitchy mood. I don't know how else to explain it, but I'm learning how to fight it. And I think you all can agree that's exactly what I need. I have to do it before we go on the tour, where I'm sure things are going to be just as hard, if not worse." She cast her eyes around the group, noticing their nods of agreement.

"I also know that most of you don't believe me, but I wasn't drunk when those pictures were taken. Yes, I went to the bar. I was pissed off. Yes, I ordered a drink and told him to leave the bottle. And yeah, I touched the glass and thought about drinking it, but I didn't." Her voice took on a quiver, "I was sick the next day; plain old sick, not hung over."

"It's ok," Brian responded softly. "We're not mad at you. At least I'm not. I feel pretty responsible for what happened."

Tori stared at him, "Why's that?"

He shrugged slightly, searching for the words. Leaning forward in his chair, he placed his elbows on his knees, "Well, I knew how hard this life could be, and I did everything I could to bring you into it." He hung his head, hands grasping one another in front of his face, "It was pretty selfish of me."

Michael grunted aloud, causing Brian to look up, nodding at his brother-in-law. *Yeah, I know, you tried to warn me, but I wasn't listening;* he spoke to the other man telepathically. "Anyways," he straightened in his seat, "You're here, and we all want to do whatever we can to help you be successful."

The remainder of the group quickly echoed his sentiments, and Tori smiled, fairly certain they felt genuine concern. "Thanks, guys, I really appreciate it, and I'll do my best to keep up with your crazy lifestyle."

Standing, the meeting adjourned, and the couple was left alone in their room. Moving over to the window, she looked out across the sparkling lights below them, a little sadness eating at her gut. *Enrique has been keeping his distance so that I feel better, so why is it that I actually feel worse?* She missed him, only having the thought bring a wave of guilt. *Damn, why am I still stuck here? I shouldn't feel this way after all this time.*

Michael had been keeping himself at bay as well, and it occurred to her that it had been over a week since they had been intimate. She couldn't remember the last time she had gone so long without. *Had to have been before we were married.* She released a deep sigh, *nope. It was after he burned himself in Florida, when we had our first little dispute.*

Quietly, Michael slipped up behind his wife, sliding his arms around her waist. "What are you thinking about, love?" he cooed softly through her hair.

Running her hands along his arms, she smiled softly, "Trying to remember the last time we made love." He made an odd sound, and she pulled herself free enough to turn and look at him, "What's that for?"

"I'm not sure you're up for making love," he whispered as he smoothed her hair. "I'm not even sure what to think anymore." He leaned his forehead against hers, desperate to avoid stressing her any further.

"Are you saying you don't want to be with me?" her voice cracked, dripping with sadness.

"Come on, you know that's not what I meant. I'm... worried about you. I love you so much..." his voice trailed away, his hands moving over her body. "I'm really sorry I didn't believe you about Enrique, either."

Tori stiffened, "Why do you say that? Did you *ask* him?"

"No, I didn't ask him!" he coughed a laugh at the question. "I decided I wasn't being fair to you. I mean, it's almost like our fight was the straw. You know the one that broke the camel's back. So I'm more than satisfied you were telling the truth. Besides, that makes it essentially my fault, and I hate that. But, at least you're on the mend."

Tori's smile flickered, her hand moving up to run along the line of his jaw and hold him at the nape of his neck, her thumb caressing his ear, "I'm fine, love. And it's not your fault or anyone's fault really. I got sick. That means I'll get better." Leaning her brow against his once more, she whispered hoarsely, "Make love to me?"

Giving her a small chuckle, he grasped her more firmly, "You know I'm always up for making love to my wife." His voice cracked slightly at the words *my wife,* the emotion they held for him evident.

Lifting her chin, she kissed him, her hands searching for the edges of his shirt so she could remove it, "Well, then," she admonished quietly, "What the hell are you waiting for?"

Kiss and Make Up

Within in a few minutes, they were both naked, stretched out on their bed. Running his hands over her body, he noticed that she tensed when he grasped her breast, his thumb sliding over his name. "You really ok?" he demanded gently.

"Yeah, just tender, that's all," she focused on relaxing her features that had shifted into a frown.

Michael slid his hands smoothly over her skin, then parting her legs he pushed his way inside her. Kissing and nuzzling her neck, he breathed into her ear, catching her leg and raising it to gain fuller access to her wet interior. She had seemed eager when they first began, but he could sense a shift in her emotions and her desire ebbed rapidly.

Tori felt a stab of pain as he moved, her brow crinkling in confusion. Clawing at his back, she drew deep breaths, refusing to acknowledge the discomfort being with him produced. She wanted this, wanted to show him that she loved him. So why was her body refusing to cooperate?

Continuing, he pushed harder, doing his best to satisfy her in the darkness, and becoming driven to finish by the slight sound of a whimper. Holding himself over her in the dim glow, small drops of sweat glistened on her forehead, her features drawn and no longer enjoying their the activity.

He stared down into her crystal blue eyes, while sad thoughts drew lines into his forehead. He could feel fear in his gut, afraid that she lay with him, but she really wasn't his anymore. He had no evidence that she had been with the other man, and she had been ill for days, which didn't sit well with him either. She seemed to be on an emotional roller coaster, and was dragging him along with her for every bump along the way.

Bending over to kiss her pretty lips, he whispered his affection and then slid off to the side, not bothering with a shower. Facing the wall, he pulled the covers tighter against him and waited to see what his wife would do. It came as no surprise that she turned her back on him, staring out the window, and he listened to the calmness of her breathing until he fell asleep.

Tori lay still, waiting for him to lose consciousness, and allowed a small sigh of relief when it finally happened. She had been turning her ring on her finger, and slid it out to the end to toy with it in the faint light that shone in through the panes of glass. Slithering out of the sheets, she stepped over to stare down at the glimmer of cars and streetlamps covering the ground below.

Heaving another cleansing breath, her mind turned, her thoughts roaming over the last few weeks and months. She knew she was still plagued by the physical urges, the ones that had provoked her husband to send her into the arms of another. *'Don't make love to that man,'* he had said. *Does he have any idea how much those words hurt me? Or how they have torn at me?*

Of course, he didn't, and wouldn't either because she never said. *I'm not very good at talking,* she admitted to herself as she shifted her gaze to the sleeping figure across the room. *You show him the angry... you never show him the pain.* A tear slipped from her eye, and she wiped at it crossly,

167

oh, now you wanna cry? What the hell is the matter with you? Can't think straight, overly emotional, tired, lost?

She felt annoyed at the conundrum that seemed to be playing havoc with her health. On Christmas morning, Enrique had walked back into her life, throwing her heart and mind into chaos. *That's the straw that broke the camel's back, love, not you.* She would like to blame her mate for her conflicting thoughts, but in the end her husband's choice to look the other way only added fuel to the smoldering fire.

Leaning her head against the glass, she continued to watch him, barely able to make out the rise and fall of the blanket as Michael slept. *He's here for you. You know he would do damn near anything for you.* Another tear, and this time she let it drip. *You're such a stupid bitch. Your life is perfect. It's whatever you want it to be, and you can't even decide. And you damn sure don't love him enough.*

Moving into the bathroom, Tori closed the door quietly and turned on a cold shower. Stepping beneath the gentle spray, she washed the streaks from her face, then lay her cheek against the wall.

The air moving across her lips in deep puffs, a wave of nausea hit. She recalled the night she had lied to him about being ill. *The night Mason Hunt touched me and sent me into a tither.* It had been a lie then, but tonight she thought she might actually vomit. *Karma come to get me.*

That's another time I had proven myself to be unworthy of him; she judged herself harshly at the way she had used her husband to satisfy her physical impulses. *The needs the other man awoke inside me.*

Resting her hand against the wall, she stared at her ring. *For Tori, love of my life.* She couldn't see the words, but she knew they were there. *Why? Why does he care about you so fucking much? You... don't... deserve it.*

She cut off the torrent and reached for her towel, her

hand trembling as she did so. She was tired of playing the game, exhausted at always putting on her show; keeping up her façade. *I'm ready for the real. How I really feel. What I really want. What is it that I really want?*

Her flesh pimpled from her cool shower, she placed her palms flat on the counter and leaned forward; the cloth draped across her back, she stared at herself in the mirror.

Her scar glared back at her, taunting her. Her mind racing, it leapt to the photograph that Eddie had taken of her when it was fresh. She had discovered the ragged picture in Michael's wallet not long ago when she was snooping.

She had been shocked to find it there, and even more so that Eddie had sent it to him. *A threat, perhaps? Or to brag, more like.* Her husband had kept it, the only personal item among the contents. *Jesus, how many times, and how many ways, do you have to see it? That man loves you. More than loves you.*

You could have the whole world at your feet, living this stupid crazy life with your brother. She drew a ragged breath, *but you are the whole world to Michael.* Pulling open the door abruptly, she was startled to discover him standing outside of it.

"What the hell are you doing?" he demanded with a hint of anger.

Eyes wide, she struggled to breathe, her lip quivering wildly. Reaching for him, she grabbed and held his warm flesh against her. "Nothing, baby."

She ran her hands up to the nape of his neck, finding the sandy curls with the tips of her fingers, "Could you just… hold me?" She could feel his tension as she clung to him, and knew she had upset him, again.

However, he complied, and his muscular arms wound around her. "Like this?" he breathed into her hair.

"Tighter," her voice trembled, "Like you won't ever let

me go."

He laughed quietly, sliding and shifting his hold to get a better grip, hands moving up her back beneath her dark, damp waves. "You have any idea how much I love you?" he whispered. "There's no chance of my *ever* letting you go."

Her palms going sweaty, Tori swallowed hard. *Damn. I love him so much. Need him like I've never needed anyone.* Taken with the urge to express her feelings, she wanted to say *I love you.* But words weren't enough and never had been.

The only language of love she really spoke, the only one she really knew, was the one that didn't use words; the one her body knew. Caressing his neck, kissing at his ear and blowing warm air against the curls that covered it. "Please, Michael," she choked, barely audible as she pushed him back towards the bed.

Allowing her to take the lead, he half expected her to grow anxious, and use him in the angry fashion that had become her norm. To his surprise, she didn't climb on top of him as she laid him back onto the sheets. Instead, her firm hands shifted into caresses of silk as they glided across him, tickling the hairs of his chest and sliding down the thin line that marked the path from his belly button to the portion hidden by his jeans.

Already naked, he relaxed and allowed her tendrils to explore him, as if it were the first time she had ever touched him. Lips soft, she kissed the delicate skin, sliding her bare flesh down his legs as she made her way until she found his hardness and grasped it firmly. A low moan escaped him, her tongue making its way around the tip of him in a slow, teasing circle.

It had been months it seemed since she had played this part, and she was consumed by the urge to do her very best; to use her skill to convey to him the things her heart cried to be exposed, things she longed so deeply for him to know. The things no amount of languages and no amount of words could reveal. This was all that she had, all that she knew, and all that she could do. This is what she was good at.

While pushing back more deeply into the pillow, Michael's hands found their way to her head, weaving through the dark curls so that he could massage her scalp as she pleased him. Closing his eyes, he felt the waves wash over him when she pushed him down her throat, working him in and out of her mouth, her cajoling fingers massaging the flesh at the base of him and finding their way to the sensitive ridges below.

Mouth open wide, he panted at the sensations her touch produced, calling her name quietly, not to distract her from the place she was taking him. Her hands on his hips, grasping him, clawing for a moment, his urgency became overpowering as her firm, rasping movements pushed him over the edge and his full body began to tremble, him expecting her to pull away.

Holding her position, Tori drank him in and allowed him to remain inside of her as she guided him through his fulfillment. Rubbing the length of him with firm fingers, she continued to lick and tease, a small smile dancing on her lips.

Her toying delayed his softening, and she continued to catch him with a mock biting motion, overjoyed at the sounds he had produced and the expression that had contorted his face as she worked him.

Eventually relinquishing her grasp, she slid her body up along his, stretching out next to him, pressing the front of her bare skin against his side. Catching the sheet, she draped it lightly across them, and dug her fingers firmly into the pelt that coated his chest and obscured her name.

Michael allowed her to fawn over him for several minutes; fingers tantalizing his tingling flesh from neck to hip, and back again. His breath returning to normal, he caught her fingers and laced them with his own. Fighting to keep his words in line, his tone soft, "That was… surprising."

"Yeah," she agreed, keeping her eyes focused on the nipple she had been teasing. "I'm sorry."

"Sorry?" he couldn't keep the shock from his voice, and he shifted to hold her more tightly, "Sorry for what, baby girl?"

"I don't love you enough," she answered too quickly. Pausing, she allowed the words to turn in her mind for a moment. "What I mean is; I don't say it enough. I don't show you… enough." A tear unexpectedly dropped from her eye, wetting his skin, and she sniffed slightly, not wanting to let on that she was crying by wiping at it, in case he didn't know.

Michael had felt the droplet, and it startled him. Shifting slowly, he pushed his wife over onto her back, swiping her tresses away from her face. Catching her jaw with the tips of his fingers, he searched her misty blue eyes, looking for the truth he knew was hidden in them somewhere.

A second tear slipped from her eye, and he caught it, wiping it against her temple, "Why do you hide that you cry?" His voice tender, no anger or accusation to be found, "You know that you are safe here… with me. I would never do anything to hurt you."

"I know," she nodded slightly, "But tears are for the weak."

Licking his lip, her husband adjusted himself, his flesh sticking to hers suddenly uncomfortable. "Who told you that?" he demanded, his voice only slightly raised, almost certain he already knew.

Her lip quivered, but she couldn't bring herself to speak his name. "I know it isn't true, ok? But it's hard for me. I wish that I could make you understand."

"You don't have to make me do anything. I already do, don't you see? Better than you will ever know." He pressed his palm firmly against her, running his hand up and down between her ribs and her thigh. Leaning over, he laid his forehead against hers and closed his eyes. Drawing a deep breath, he exhaled it slowly, aware that she trembled as he held her.

"We gotta hang on, ya know? You and me… we're a great team. Meant to be, we are. Don't ever doubt it. Don't ever forget it." He kissed her nose, his right hand leaving her hip to smooth her hair. "Promise me, baby girl. Promise me you will always hang on?"

Keeping her eyes closed, she could feel his breath on her face as he spoke. His words reminded her of Enrique, and the first time anyone had ever spoken to her in that way. The first time she had ever been a part of *you and me*. But this time was different; she could feel it in her gut. "I promise," she whispered in return, hoping that it was true and she would never forget to hang on.

Return of the Fury

Michael awoke the next morning to find his bride still pressed against him, with the sun peeking through the window, laying a soft glow across her delicate features. Nuzzling her gently, he used his fingers to trace the line of her until awoke enough to part her legs, and he could make his way inside.

Kissing and holding him, Tori felt relieved to find that the discomfort of the previous night had disappeared, and she could accept him in full. Wrapping her legs around him, she grunted and moaned, quite happy to be his wife and share his bed and his life. Looking up into his creamy brown orbs, she wished for a brief moment that they were back in a small town, in a giant house, and the day would be theirs to do with as they pleased.

Making their way into the bathroom afterwards, the couple showered and toweled off, sharing smiles and lover's banter. Leaving her to her morning routine, Michael dressed, calling that he would see her downstairs in the restaurant. Peeking his head through the door, he prodded, "Is that ok?"

"Sure," she smiled, "Half an hour or so."

He grinned back at her, "Take your time, baby girl." Slapping the door frame with an open palm as a farewell, he exited the room, whistling while he made his way down the hall.

Slipping on her bra and panties, Tori's mind churned. An odd, euphoric state had settled over her, and she prodded herself not to ruin it, and to simply hang on. Pulling out the container as part of her morning ritual, she stared down at the rows of plastic. She noted that the prescription was almost gone, and would have to be refilled after her trip to see the doctor.

A small smile curled her lips as she contemplated the return visit, now only a few weeks away. *After that, we get to try for a baby. If we want to, that is.* Staring down at the near empty cartridge, her smile slowly faded, *damn, second sugar pill. I'll start today.*

Deciding to put on a pad, she prepared for the arrival of her monthly visitor and pursed her lips at the irony. *I never thought menstruating was such a pain, until I started getting them all the time.* That taken care of; she threw on her clothes and went to cover her face before making her way downstairs.

Michael sat in the dining room, impatiently watching the door for her entrance.

Smiling, she took her seat at the extravagant table and cooed, "Did you order?"

"Yeah," he stood slightly to allow her to move into her chair, "I got you the usual."

Taking their time, the couple discussed the day's agenda, expecting to have at least another hour before any of the other band members turned up. Tori could see the surprised expression cross her husband's face before her brother grabbed the chair next to her, "Hey, guys, come on; we gotta go."

Frowning, Tori demanded in a sharp tone, "What the hell, Danny? Go where? I didn't expect to see you up and about this early," the confusion clear on her painted features.

"Terry called my room. There's been some trouble. We need to get over to your friend's house, ASAP," he panted, slightly out of breath in his rush to speak.

Tori's heart froze, "What kind of trouble?"

"He didn't say," he waved his hand at them as he spoke. "He just said to get over to the Tates' right now."

Standing, the couple waved to the waiter so that he would add the bill to their room's tab, and quickly made their way to the exit. Outside, Brian had already called for the car, and the three of them piled inside. "Where's Collin and Cody?"

"I didn't wake them. They each had girls with them last night, and I don't figure they will want to be disturbed. Besides, we don't have time to wait on them," he leaned back into the seat, trying to mask his disheveled appearance by re-buttoning his shirt.

"Are those the same clothes you had on yesterday?" she demanded, concerned that he had slept in them. "Didn't you have a girl with you last night as well?"

Staring out the window, he ran a hand through his nearly black hair, "No, I didn't, not that it's any of your business." He shifted his eyes over at her briefly, nervously aware of the fit she would throw if she knew who lay in his bed.

The three of them rode in an uneasy silence, and Michael reached over to take his wife's hand. Massaging it gently, he toyed with her ring, giving her a reassuring grin when she looked his way. "Relax, baby girl," he prodded her gently in German.

Giving him a squeeze, she only nodded. The half-way house being quite a distance from their luxury hotel, it took the better part of an hour for them to traverse the distance in the morning rush of cars and people. Staring through the glass, Tori could see a dark cloud of smoke hanging on the horizon, looming larger as they drew closer to their target.

The dark smudge lingered, spoiling her mood as they

drew closer. It had not moved, and only seemed to be dissipating, yet still hanging in the area where the massive Victorian stood. They had visited the stately structure only a week before, and the sight of the smoke in the air above the vicinity put her on edge.

"What do you suppose that is?" she finally indicated the thinning wisps when she couldn't hold her thoughts in any longer.

Michael had noticed it as well, and sighed relief that she had finally spoken up, as he had not wanted to be the one to point it out, "I'm sure it's nothing," he reassured, thick lines furrowing his brow.

Making the last turn before the house, it became apparent that it was, in fact, *not* nothing, and the fire engine still sat in front of the lot. Exiting the limo halfway down the block, Tori broke into a dead run, headed for the house, or what had been left of it. Tears on her cheeks, she pulled up short, staring at the smoldering embers of the first true home she had ever known.

A hand clamped onto her shoulder, spinning her around abruptly, and she found herself staring into Brett's green eyes, "What the fuck are you doin'? You damn well know you don' go nowhere without us!"

"How the hell did you find us?" she stammered, utterly shocked to see him.

"We jumped in a cab an' followed you." Tightening his grip on her, he lifted his chin towards the catastrophe, "When did this happen?"

"We don't know. Brian came down to get us, and we left in a rush. I'm sorry we didn't let you know." She looked over at him, relieved that he didn't appear to be too angry at her lapse in judgment. Swallowing hard, she wiped her face, "We didn't even know it was a fire until we got here."

At that moment, they were joined by Terry, who pointed

off to the side, "Everyone escaped. They're all gathered over there."

Pushing their way through the light crowd, Tori found the Tates, along with the rest of the residents, gathered at the back of an ambulance. They were being examined and treated as needed, most of them in a state of undress or night clothing. Sharon stood wrapped in a blanket, and the two women were immediately crying, clinging to one another tightly.

"Oh my God," Tori breathed, "I was so scared."

"I know," her friend replied weakly, "But we're ok. We got out, and that's what matters."

Holding the shorter woman loosely around the shoulders, "What the hell happened?" she demanded.

Taking a step back, Sharon didn't reply. Staring at the young woman she had nurtured like a daughter, she pressed her lips together tightly, causing the skin below her lower lip to dimple heavily. Drawing air in deeply through her nose, she finally murmured, "They think it was arson."

Tori's jaw dropped, and she spun around wildly, her eyes taking in the crowd around them. *Arson!* If that were true, they were in trouble. And not just a little bit of trouble, either. The kind of trouble that only leads to one thing. Her mind racing, she knew they needed to act fast.

"I need a phone," she stammered.

"See, I told you that you guys needed a cell phone," Brian admonished as he handed her his device.

"That won't be necessary," Eli stated as he reached out to prevent her from using it.

Her mouth hanging open for the second time, Tori shifted her eyes up and down the man before her, "Holy shit, what the hell are you doing here?"

"Disobeying orders," he stated flatly, "And we need to talk. But not here. We need to move away from this crowd

178

and get to a more secure location."

"Yes, let's move to the shop," Terry agreed, already nervous at the number of strangers surrounding them.

Piling into the limo, the group moved the ten blocks to the store in short order, Tori noting that Mason Hunt was among them as they entered the shop. Giving her a quick glance, he did not meet her gaze, and she understood that their meeting should remain a secret.

Moving everyone to the back of the store, Terry quickly moved to put Enrique on guard at the double doors, "That way we will have some warning if anyone comes looking for us."

"That's not good enough," Michael interceded, "Lock the doors. Get these customers out of here, and don't let anyone else in."

Terry stared at the younger man for a moment, then nodding, moved to comply. Returning a few minutes later, he found the group scattered about his small work area, a motley crew at best. "Doors are locked," he announced.

Tori glanced around the small gathering, taking everyone in. The Tates had been cleared by the EMT and had come with them after only a small amount of prodding. The rest of their household had remained behind, so it was herself, Michael, and Brian, along with the couple, her newest bodyguards and the three FBI agents, counting the retired one.

"So," she demanded gruffly as she glared at the group, "Does anyone actually have anything concrete, as far as information goes? Or is it all supposition?"

Eli cocked his head at her, "Boy, you've gotten mouthy. How about a little respect?"

Tori glowered at him. "Someone burned down their house," she opened a palm towards the couple. "We're lucky no one was killed. If you know something about this, I suggest you speak up, right the fuck now!"

Clenching his jaw, Eli could feel his neck flush with rage. "You know, I'm not sure what I ever actually saw in you," he spit the words at her, disturbed that she had become so different from the quiet and meek girl that he remembered.

"Yeah, well that makes two of us," she stood up taller so she could look down at him. "What the hell is going on, Eli. Stop beating around the bush and tell us what you know," she called out loudly, aware that the man always seemed to be around when there was trouble.

"We don't know anything," Mason cut in. "Well, not much of anything."

Tori looked over at him, still unsure if she should know him or not. "Ok, so tell me what you do know."

Cutting his eyes over at the woman, still wrapped in a blanket, he shook his head. Switching to French, he spoke in a low tone, "They found you. And Eli's right, we're disobeying orders by speaking to you."

"So what does that mean exactly," she lowered her voice as well.

"It means we all have to make a choice at some point. Everyone does. We're choosing to take your side," he shrugged. "In the end, it will probably cost both our jobs, if not our lives."

The girl stared at him, unsure how to react to his choice of words.

Seeing his wife at a loss, Michael hijacked the conversation with a grimace, "Yeah, we can all see how deeply concerned about everything the Feds have been." His voice dripped with accusation, and it clearly took the newest agent in the room by surprise.

"You know, I don't believe we've met. I'm Mason Hunt, Special Agent if you will," he held out his hand as he spoke.

Michael stared down at the extension, unsure if he were

actually going to shake it. Rocking his jaw side to side, he slowly raised his right appendage to grasp the other man firmly, "I would say pleased to meet you, but that remains to be seen."

Mason laughed out loud, "Yes, I can see you are very protective of your wife. I know you're probably not aware of it, but we've been shadowing you guys for a while." He stopped short when Michael's expression failed to change and glanced over at his partner. "Well, maybe you are aware," he stated less confidently and swung his gaze to stare at the girl.

Nodding, Tori bit her lip, "Yup, secrets and lies. That's all Feds are good for."

"Now wait a minute," Mason held up his right hand. "Let's be very clear here. The enemy is out there. If we're going to get anywhere, we all need to agree that we're on the same side."

"Are we?" Tori cut in sharply. "From what I've seen, the Feds are a group in name only, and it's pretty much every man for himself." Eli hung his head slightly as she spoke, and she carried on, "You want me to cooperate, you're going to have to do better than that."

Looking over at the soot smeared faces of Brandon and Sharon Tate, Agent Hunt shook his head. "Terry, is there some place we can take these two? I mean someplace safe where they can get cleaned up and get some rest?"

"I can take them to our hotel," Brian offered quickly, "Get them some clothes, too. Whatever they need." Tori stared at her brother, aware that his generosity might have been due to her connection to the couple, but she would take it, either way.

"Thanks, Danny, that would be great," she mumbled as she stepped over to give him a hug. "I'll get to the bottom of this and see you later, ok?" He stared at her, aware that her mood had changed, which frightened him.

"Yeah, sure thing, sis. I'll take good care of them. And I'll send the car back after you, in case you need a ride." Wrapping his arms around his sibling, he hugged her tightly, while hoping the fear that danced in the pit of his stomach didn't show. Backing away a moment later, he curled his fingers to indicate for them to follow him out to the limo, and Terry moved to act as their escort.

"I'm going with them," he stated in a crisp voice. "Keep me informed should anything happen," well aware that there were more people needing looked after than eyes to do the looking at the moment.

Tori watched the swinging doors sway after the four had passed through them. Drawing a deep breath, she could almost feel the tension drawing in around her, aware that the danger had always been there. She had known it for a while, since she woke up in Mercy hospital in fact. But she kept hoping at some point, it would simply go away.

Fated

Tori glanced around at the familiar room, riddled with guilt, "I shouldn't have been here. This is my fault." She shook her head at the five men who shared the space with her.

"Your fault?" Eli countered flatly, "You're damn right, it's your fault. But not for the reason you think." She glared at him, chest beginning to heave visibly. "You think things would have been different if you were still hiding in that little town in Texas," he accused.

"Yeah, exactly. If I hadn't been drawn in, they wouldn't have found me," she spit out, anger simmering and leaking into her voice. "If I hadn't allowed them to persuade me, to put my picture out and advertise where to find me, this wouldn't have happened."

"Sure, it would have, it just wouldn't have happened here," he lifted his chin slightly as he spoke. "They got to Doug, Tori. I saw the pictures. What they did to him; it was beyond horrific. They know where you have been, and probably everything about you, from the beginning. If you hadn't surfaced here, they would have gone after you there."

Staring at a bench strewn with tools, her mind raced. *If they had hit the town, oh my God. They could have hurt or killed... everyone. Done it just to prove a point.* "Wow, they

183

aren't going to give up, are they…"

Eli could see the pain on her face, the awareness that she wasn't going to get out of the task that had been waiting for her to complete. "I don't think so. I think that it has always been your fate. That you would have to deal with this. Or it would deal with you."

Her crystal eyes shifting, she met his gaze, and the words of his note flowed through her troubled thoughts. She could see them through her mind's eye as if she held his book in her hand, and the message that it held. The special words her friend had penned:

> *My Dearest Tori,*
>
> *I know the past was filled with difficult times, and your future feels uncertain. Understand that you are not alone in your quest and that even though your path will not be an easy one, you are strong, and you will endure, so long as you endeavor to persevere. My thoughts and hopes are with you.*
> *Yours Always,*
> *Eli*

My future feels uncertain, but it isn't. It's been waiting for me to accept it, and to take my final role. Swinging her focus around the small group that stood staring at her, they were patiently waiting for her to decide what to do next. *I have been such a fool.* Clenching her jaw, her anger no longer simmered; it had hit hard boil. "Well then, I guess I have a job to do."

Lifting her chin towards Brett and Enrique, "Looks like I could use your help after all. Are you with me?"

"Oh, hell yeah," Enrique jumped at the chance, more than eager to whisk her away and delve into the mayhem once more.

"I'm coming too," Michael interjected, not about to be left behind this time.

Tori inhaled sharply, as if she had been kicked. Turning to her mate, she reached out to him, her heart torn at the realization this could be their last time ever to speak to one another. She shook her head, "I can't let you do that, love. I need you to stay here. I need you to watch my brother and my friends, make sure they stay safe."

"The fuck if I will," his outburst unexpected, his words sharp. "I'm going and you're not stopping me!"

Grasping his hand with her right, her left running up his arm to catch him by the neck, Tori leaned her forehead against his, "I need you here," she whispered loudly. "I need to know that you're safe and that my brother is well guarded. And I need you to come home to."

Michael reached up with his free hand, grasping her hip. Sliding it around to stroke her back, he heaved a deep sigh. "I can't let you go alone. Even with your friends. I won't stay back, and I know I can help. I know there are things we never talked about. Things I never shared with you, about my past. I'm not the nice guy you think I am."

Tori lifted her head, staring into his bits of mahogany, feeling a small wave of confusion, "What do you mean you're not a nice guy?"

Pulling away slightly, he ran his hand through his sandy waves as he tried to explain himself, and the secrets he had kept from her. Things that had scarred his soul, and that he never shared with anyone. "I was Special Forces, you know that, so you know that I have training. The same training that Henry and many of the others had. And, I was in a special unit. A unit that took care of things. Things that weren't meant to be talked about."

"I even rode with the Dragons from time to time,

working with them, while a few of them were in South America. They never said where they were, or why they were there." He paused, allowing her to put two and two together, "And I didn't ask."

"I could have joined them; it was always a given that I would. I was one of them," he stared at her lips as he confessed his sins. "But when my service was up, I didn't. I walked away. I wanted a different life."

Tori shook her dark curls, her brow furrowed by pain and rage, "Then why were you there?" The night with Red came crashing in around her. "You saw what they did to me. You were there, and you didn't do anything about it?" her anger briefly found its way to him.

"No. No, baby girl, I couldn't. I wanted to take you, but Henry wouldn't let me. And he was right; Eddie would have come after us. He had to be dealt with, permanently if we were ever going to get away. My brother's plan was sound, except that Eddie got to him first. Otherwise, it would have worked."

He stared at her, the idea that he had always loved her, maybe even back then, tickling the back of his mind. "Either way, this's how it worked out. This's how it is. We can only go from here."

He drew a deep breath, separating himself from her as he prepared to make his stand, "And you're not leaving me behind. I'm your equal, capable of being as cold hearted and brutal as you are. If you're going after those bastards that run the show, I'm going with you, and not you or anyone else is going to tell me any different."

Rocky Road

Tori stared at her husband; slack-jawed at their brief altercation. She had never had him speak to her that way, and she damn sure wasn't happy that he had chosen this particular moment to stand up to her. Swallowing hard, she spoke softly, "You know, we got a rocky road ahead of us. And I don't mean because it will be dangerous. Things are going to happen. Bad things."

Michael stared into her eyes, fully aware of what she meant, "I can take it. I told you; I'm not the nice guy you think I am. I've tried to be, but in the end…" Taking another a step back, he put some more distance between them, aware that he had officially been demoted in rank from husband to underling. Glaring over at the two men in suits, he shifted to German, "We take these two with us? Or make it a group of four?"

"You're not leaving us here," Mason countered evenly, surprising the group with his linguistic abilities. Nodding towards the girl, he continued flatly, "Tori makes the calls. She's the one that knows the details. Of course, as soon as our superiors figure out that Eli and I have joined her ranks, we may get trouble from that side as well."

"Then we make sure they don't find out, don't we," Tori took charge, reverting the conversation back to a common tongue, "And we should all use English." She gave Eli a small smile, "No sense cutting out members of our own group, and it's the only language that we all speak."

"Wait a second," Enrique looked perplexed. "You means after everything that's happened, you're gonna trust this guy?" he indicated the shorter man with a waft of his hand.

Tori pursed her lips for a moment, staring at Eli's blue eyes as they met hers calmly. "Yeah," she finally agreed, "Yeah, I think I am. I can't explain to you how or why I know that we can. I just know. Ok?"

She shifted her gaze to her former lover. "Call it my sixth sense about people." She smiled, aware of all the times her intuition had paid off. "So you two need to get out of here. Give me your number though, so we can contact you when we're ready to meet up."

"We won't be far. That's our orders, to follow you around," he hesitated slightly, "Wait until they get to you and follow them back to where ever it is that they hide."

"You're kidding me. Is that really what you've been doing? Following me and waiting for them to kill me?" she stared at the first man outside the Dragons she had thought of as a friend, then shifted her gaze to his counterpart.

Mason only nodded to confirm Eli's statement, so she continued, "That son of a bitch. James Godfry made that call, didn't he? Fucking bastard, I knew he couldn't be trusted!"

Eli shifted uncomfortably and stared at the floor between his toes. "I've known for a while things weren't adding up," his voice grew quiet, "But, I didn't know what to do about it. I'm sorry." Lifting his face enough to cut his eyes up at her, he hoped he came across as sincere.

Sneak Peek at Avenged
Book 7 of A New Life Series

Eli cast a glance to his left, his partner towering above him as they marched to their sedan. "You know this is only going to get more complicated," he spoke crisply, relieved to be outside the building.

"Yes, it is," the other man agreed. "So, if you have any doubts, this is the time to speak up." Mason kept moving as he cajoled, reaching for the door handle and climbing inside.

Taking his place behind the wheel, Eli started the car and pulled away from the curb, moving a few hundred yards and parking again to wait. "You don't know her like I do," he stated flatly. "She's a compulsive liar. Only gives you enough truth to make her story sound credible."

Mason cut his gaze over at him, "Is that your ego talking?"

Drumming his fingers on the wheel, he considered the question, "I don't know. Maybe. She got the better of me, and two agents have paid the price with their lives. Three counting the one she killed when she was still with the Dragons."

"I'm going with her," his passenger cut in. "Regardless of what you think, that's the side I'm choosing. If you want to play it by the book, I will understand. But know this:

James Godfry is dirty. I can't prove it, yet. But I will."

Bending his arm, Eli slouched over and rested his elbow on the door frame, his head in his hand as if he had a migraine. "I'm tired of thinking about it. Half a decade. That's how long I've been worrying about this. Trying to figure it out."

"Stop trying so hard," Mason offered. "What's your gut telling you?"

"My *gut*?" the other man sneered, "The last time I listened to anything other than my head, I wound up reassigned. Still haven't figured out how they discovered what happened between us, either. I figure Tori talked once she was done with me." He could hear the rumble start low, turning his head to see Agent Hunt trying to suppress his laughter. "What's so fucking funny?"

"You," his counterpart continued to snicker. "I shouldn't laugh though. It took me a while to figure it out." Shifting in his seat, Mason drew a deep breath to calm his spasms, "Debra was sleeping with Godfry. I'm sure she mentioned it to him, maybe not even thinking anything of it."

"You're kidding me! How the hell did you find that out?"

"I poked around... a lot," Hunt shrugged. "Found out quite a few interesting things about the Chicago office," he dusted imaginary dirt off his knee for a moment. "The only reason I trust you, is because Tori says I can."

Eli's brow furrowed, "What the hell does that mean? You'd take her word over mine?"

"You could say that." Mason opened his left palm to the roof, "Let me clue you in on my theory about people. I don't put much stock in what people say. Everyone's a liar. Everyone hides the truth and covers their ass at some point in their lives. You want to know who someone is... what they stand for... watch what they do. They'll tell you who they are."

Mason turned enough to look the other man in the eye. "Don't judge her too harshly. In the end, she's the one who holds the key to ending this whole mess. That's a lot of weight for one pair of shoulders to bear. Besides, she didn't choose to leave you. She was holding on the best she could until she found out you were gone. That's when things fell apart."

"Yeah," Eli scoffed, "Tell me about it," leaning back into his palm with a sigh.

Get the Hell Out

Tori glanced around the shop, her lips drawn into a frown. *Son of a bitch.* She didn't want to be there. Didn't want things to have turned out the way they were. "You think the car is back yet?"

"I'll check," Brett offered calmly, leaving his cohorts in the back and making his way out to the single glass door next to the register. Pushing it open enough to glance up and down the street, he then allowed it to close, relocking it with a snap.

"Nope. Not back yet," he sighed the words when he had rejoined the others. "We should make a plan, what we're gonna do when it does get here." Glancing between the other two men, he continued, "You're in charge, baby girl. That means it's up t' you."

"This isn't a dictatorship," she tossed at him flatly, sinking down to sit on the edge of Terry's workbench.

"It ain't a democracy, neither," he replied calmly. "It's ok, tell us what you think. If we don't like it, we'll let ya know."

The girl inhaled deeply, pushing the air out noisily through a relaxed jaw, "Alrighty then." She gave them her evaluation, "We're pretty much fucked. All our bikes are scattered across the country, so we have no rides. The Organization knows everything about us, and we have almost no information on them -"

"Stop bein' negative," Brett cut her off.

"Why?" she snapped. "I'm so fucking pissed off, I can't even see straight!" her fists were clenched in her lap as she vented.

"Then take a deep breath," he stepped closer to her, his hand catching her jaw and lifting it slightly. "That's it," his thumb caressed her cheek, "Don' be angry. Be smart. We can beat these guys. You know more about 'em than you think."

Tori blinked up at him, relaxing into his touch. "We can buy some motorcycles locally, I think that will be our best option. We don't have access to much cash," her mind began to branch out. "How much was in the vault? The one here in LA?"

Brett grinned, reaching inside his jacket for his list. "Well, we inventoried 'em all, so le's see what this one has for us..." his voice trailed away as he scanned the page. "Over 400K. We could get some really nice bikes for that an' still have some t' carry aroun'."

She blinked a few times at the news. "Why did they burn the house? It doesn't make sense. They should have come to the hotel. They should have come after me."

"We'll figure it out," Michael tried to reassure her. "Brett's right. For the moment, we need to know what we're going to do. Where should we go to hole up? I don't think the hotel is a good option. Not in the long run."

"We have to separate ourselves from the group," Tori agreed, continuing his thought. "Yes, we go back to the hotel. Whatever we do needs to be dramatic and public. We need those snapping the pictures to get plenty of them so that everyone knows we aren't with the band anymore. Let's go out front, so we can leave as soon as the car gets here."

Making their way to the single glass door, Tori leaned against it, waiting impatiently for the limo. Moving up behind her, Michael ran his hand up her spine, squeezing her shoulder at the top. Turning, she leaned into his embrace and avoided looking at the others, hoping they didn't have long to wait.

Avenged is Available Now!

About the Author

Anyone who knows me could tell you, I am a friendly kind of person, never met a stranger and take up conversations anywhere at any time. I work hard, and my mind never seems to shut down, as I wake up often in the middle of the night with ideas pouring out and demanding to be dealt with. Of course that means much of my books were written in the middle of the night.

I grew up and still live in the great state of Texas where everything is bigger, where we have warm weather and a central location. I love my state, my town, and my family, which includes my four sons, my significant other, and many friends as well.

I have thoroughly enjoyed writing this story and hope that you will love reading it just as much. And of course, there will be many more adventures to come.

You can follow Samantha Jacobey at:
Website: www.SamJacobey.com
Facebook: https://www.facebook.com/SamJacobey
Twitter: https://twitter.com/SamJacobey
Pinterest: http://www.pinterest.com/samanthajacobey/

Other works by Samantha Jacobey

http://www.amazon.com/-/e/B00GEB5LX0

Summer Spirit Novella Series - no one EVER had a summer romance like this... Charlie visits another plane, parallel to our own, where Summer Angels and Dark Angels battle over the fate of man. A unique twist on an old idea that will keep you guessing; will Charlie and Clarisse ever find their HEA? (New adult)

Irrevocable Series – from affluent beginnings, BAILEY DEWITT's life has become a broken mess... after her parents died unexpectedly, she didn't think it could get any worse. But when the arrogance of man catches up and puts the entire world into a dooms-day spiral, there will be only ONE PLACE she can run to... the ONE PLACE she wanted desperately to escape.... (New Adult)

Teach Me to Prey – in this standalone thriller, JASON TRUITT and his friends have gotten their way for years. Deceit, sex, and foul play aren't normally covered in the curriculum, but they're doing whatever it takes to get under BECKY STEWART's skin. When one of the boys turns up dead, it's a race against time to save the others; a STUNNING STORY that will get your heart racing and leave you breathless by the end... (New Adult)

The Wicked Awakened – a Halloween novel, a five hundred year old witch wants to turn SARAH MATTHEWS' body into her new home... A twisted tale involving a coven hell bent on seeing that she succeeds. Who will come out on top in this epic battle of wills? (Mature read, 18+ for sexual content and violence)